COLORBLIND

Elizabeth Kidder

COLORBLIND

This story is dedicated to those who
have also experienced werifesteria,
wandering longingly through their own
Wood in search of mystery.

ONE

INTRODUCTIONS

"Do not look the beast in the eye."

I let my gaze dance away from the amber fire lurking behind those eyes, followed the curve of its spine.

"Rest your gaze on the thrashing tail, the glinting claws, but give the face only the briefest of sweeping glances."

Our gazes met, and I hurried to look away again. "If you linger in its gaze, you may be lost. It will assume all control, and you will not be able to run, even when the danger is already upon you!"

A hiss of fire escaped its mouth, and I jumped back as the crowd around us laughed and applauded. The dragon handler bowed while the bright red dragon prowled up the handler's arm to stand on his shoulder, tail curled around the man's armor protected neck.

"All deadly predators are one in the same, so be wary and cautious when approaching any of the creatures you see here today," he said. The dragon's wings flared out and beat the air a few times before settling back, the iron chain attached to the collar around its slender neck rattling. My hand instinctively reached up, and Mother's hand found it and led us away.

"What a magnificent creature," she said.

"I thought it would be bigger," said Giselle, as she skipped around us in her new sea foam green lace dress. I felt the hem of my favorite indigo blue dress on my open slippers, and wondered when I would get a grown-up dress, like my eldest sister, as well as the heeled shoes, with the height difference between us even more pronounced. We used to share everything, but when Giselle turned thirteen last month, her body suddenly changed, as though trying to keep pace with her mental maturity, and she received a brand new wardrobe. She knew that I felt left behind, and came over to hold my free hand, which I was too old for, being very nearly ten, but I let her do it anyway.

"The larger dragons are too difficult to train, and very nearly extinct besides," said an informed voice behind us. I turned to see Rose keeping pace, her nose so far in an open book it would get caught if it was suddenly snapped shut, which I considered doing for a moment. Mother paused, and I wonder if I spoke that thought out loud. But she only turned to say, "Come along, Rosalind darling." She did with a startled look when her book bumped into Giselle's back. Giselle sighed and arched up our connected hands so Rose could come through and walk in front of us, preventing any more accidental run-ins.

The walkway around us was filled with men and women of society, flanked on either side by hedges that were too tall for me to see over. Giselle could though, in her new heels, and described the maze of a garden we walked through, filled with dragons, chimeras, griffins and other creatures she could not name. Every year the traveling menagerie brought strange, new creatures, along with the crowd favorites, like the aquarium filled with miniature sea horses with manes like sea foam, their front halves hoofed like their land counterparts, their back halves finned and scaled. Then there were the unicorn riders, beautiful dark haired virgins who leapt and twirled on the backs of their unicorns, who move gracefully, but with hidden power, their horns sharp as swords.

The traveling menagerie had been a yearly tradition as long as I could remember, since before I could even walk. Some of my earliest memories were of looking out through the frilled curtains of my pram at the strange beasts and strange faces, while Giselle walked alongside, pointing at man and beast alike and saying words I didn't yet understand. We had our favorites. Giselle longed to become a unicorn rider someday, and would often make us wait till after the last show to go and admire the glowing mounts up close. Rose enjoyed studying the animals with magic properties, the fiery salamanders and the ravens that dispensed darkness from their wings when they flew. But I had always liked the predators best, the white tigers and jewel-toned dragons, the dreadwolves, large as lions with louder roars. These hunters were unlike anything else, vast, powerful, a mystery onto themselves.

The elite of our city swirled about us in finery and lilting voices, charming me almost as much as the exotic creatures. My mother's friends approached us with exclamations at our growth and beauty, gossip over the latest scandal, and inquiries at our father's whereabouts and wellbeing. Our father was wealthy, even among the high society we surrounded ourselves with. He was a merchant of the highest degree, as close to the royal family as a man of business could be. He sent out his ships and caravans to trade at the farthest reaches of our kingdom, and he always came out on top. He used his vast wealth to provide his wife and three daughters with every luxury. We lived in a large city, the center of trade and commerce, where the streets bustled with clip-clop horse hooves and whir of carriage wheels, the sharp tap of ladies heels and the clicks of canes. Our house was built of marble and copper, the many windows gleaming in the sun from their daily washings. Inside, the cool stone was muffled with rugs and tapestries. The oaken staircase led up to our private quarters, each room with its own fireplace. We had a battalion of maids, an army of servants, to keep our mansion running and our needs and desires met. Dresses made with lace and silk, bejeweled shoes and hair combs, enough jewelry to make us glitter even in the darkest night, perfumes from exotic lands that smelled of unknown fruits and spices, and living quarters fit for a princess. In fact, when visiting the castle during the off months when the court was moved to the summer palace, the tour had revealed the princesses' rooms to be much like our own.

I knew very little about my father. He had built his empire of trade from the ground up, and remained involved in all aspects of his business, from the wagon trains to the ship manifests, from the inspection of goods to the apprentices and hired hands under him. His level of dedication kept him away from home most months of the year. We only saw him at the most important of occasions, or at evening meals in between his trips; most of his days at home were spent in his private quarters.

Giselle and I gravitated naturally towards our mother, light of every conversation and the patience of a saint. When most women turned over their children to governesses and maids until they were old enough to care for themselves, our mother remained involved with our upbringing, offering valuable lessons in subjects not covered by our tutors, like using words as weapons or bridges, speaking both sincerity and flattery, valuable tools for making our way in society. Our mother introduced us all into society at a very young age, and I was quickly bedazzled and charmed by the colors, the lights, the tinkling of glasses and quick strums of violins. Every time my mother told us of a new soiree, I'd spend hours putting together the outfit I would wear, my maidservant indulging me as I draped myself in chiffon scarves and ropes of pearls, my hair haphazardly pinned as I attempted to walk in Giselle's heels, without her knowledge of course, before Mother would come in and set my appearance to rights with experienced hands before she, Giselle and I left for the next party. She would ask Rose to come along, so her mother could introduce her beautiful daughter to all of her friends. But she'd simply shake her head and return to whatever book had recently grabbed her attention. Our mother would look at her with a sad smile, place a gentle hand on her head, and usher the rest of us out to the waiting carriage.

The menagerie was one of the few places that Rose came along with us to, much less showed any interest in. When she wasn't reading about the creatures we saw, she was writing notes in a journal, much to the amazement of others witnessing a seven-year-old question a handler about the diet of the unicorns, and then informing him that the moonbeam plants they were feeding them were too ripe and needed to be cut closer to the full moon to ensure a healthier coat and a stronger performance.

All too soon, the last unicorn was led away, the doors closed on the caravans, and the sun sank behind the nearest buildings, casting our exit into shadow as we made our way to our waiting carriage and began the trip home. Giselle and Mother sat together facing Rosalind and I, engaged in conversation. In the dim light, the two looked so similar, the way they held themselves, laughing at jokes I didn't understand. I turned to Rosalind, haloed in the illuminated carriage window. "Rose?"

"Yes, Evelyn?" she said, face not leaving her book.

"Do you ever wish you were older?"

"We'll all be older soon enough," she said pragmatically. "You are older than you were when the day began."

I sighed. Sometimes, Rose's smart answers annoyed me to no end. Giselle couldn't stand Rose's book smarts, but she was nearly six years Rose's elder, and I think there was a little jealousy on Giselle's part of the kind of quiet power Rose had, content in her own knowledge and none other. It was that honesty I liked. Beyond her fount of information, she always gave a truthful opinion to any question I asked.

"I don't mean eventually, I mean now. Do you ever wish to skip everything and get to the end?"

At this, she looked up from her book at me, sunlight bouncing off her golden hair. "I think I understand what you mean," she says, slowly, and I know she's thinking through her next words. "Sometimes, when I'm reading a book, and the characters are in an awful state, waylaid or injured or mourning, I want so terribly to turn to the final pages and see how everything ended, even if I know it ends badly, just to be done with it. But, I think it's important that you keep going through, page by page, because even if things are bad, it's worth it to learn more about them, and about yourself. Then, at the end, you've earned the victory, or learned from the defeat. Does that make sense to you?"

"Yes, I think so. I think…you're saying that I'm going to be defeated?"

She laughed, a child's laugh so unlike the way she spoke. "I'm saying that life has to be lived. You can't skip to the end, and even if you could, I don't think it would be worth it."

"I suppose you're right."

"I know I am," she said matter-of-factly, and returned to her book.

TWO

PARTY

When I was thirteen, Giselle held her first party, her debut, a gathering to announce to the members of society that she was sixteen and ready to join their ranks. I had heard it was a wonderful party, attended by the most elite and high ranking of the city. There had been a banquet fit for the king, wonderful music and dancing late into the night, and everyone had commented on how beautiful the eldest sister was, including the many eligible young men that had attended. It was then that I learned what eligible meant to me, to my family, to my future.

I was not allowed to attend the debut, and the morning after, while Giselle was still sleeping off the success of last night, my mother came in to tell me why. The importance of the debut on your sixteenth birthday was that not only did you join society, but you were also of an age to accept suitors and court. Our mother and father had met at our mother's debut, and not a year later they were married. My mother always spoke so fondly of our father, the sweetness with which he'd courted her, the small intimate tokens they'd exchanged, the whispered secrets shared in the garden. I loved to hear my mother's tales, and after learning about the eligible men that would be at my own debut, I slowly started to alter the tales to fit my own dreams. I fantasized about what we would both be wearing when our eyes met across the ballroom floor, what dance would whirl us across the floor under the approving gaze of everyone, especially my mother and father, his promise to call on me within the week. I was besotted with my eligible young man, and I began to plan my debut with growing anticipation.

After years of waiting, I was finally rewarded, and awoke earlier than my maid on the morning of my sixteenth birthday, laying out jewelry and ribbons at my vanity until she arrived. We looked at each other in the mirror, discussing arrangement and placement as she teased and pinned and lifted my hair into an elegant upsweep, loose ringlets cascading down my head to brush the nape of my neck. She wove sapphire blue ribbons into my curls, and I gave her a simple circlet to tuck around the gathered hair on the crown of my head.

My mother entered then, and my maid quietly departed. I turned around to face her, and the beaming smile she gave me suppressed my growing anxiety. "You look absolutely beautiful, my Evelyn," she told me, and wrapped me in her embrace. She smelled of lavender, as always, and I took a little courage from this familiarity. She must have felt the erratic thumping of my heart, and she laughed.

"Peace, my daughter. Everything is going as planned, you have nothing to worry about." I gave a brave smile, small yet determined, and attempted to breathe deeply.

I was served a light lunch of cheese and fruit, and then it was time to put on my dress. It was brand new, just for this occasion, a beautiful profusion of rich blue fabrics. The bodice was embellished with tiny winking diamonds so subtle that they gave the impression of a starry night, even in the bright afternoon sun. The skirt seemed endless, like a waterfall cascading around my feet. After I had put on the petticoat and corset, I stepped carefully into the dress, and stood straight as my maid began tightening the stays. As her hands flew deftly behind me, rhythmically pulling the ties, I looked outside the window. The sun was beginning its downward descent, the blue sky ever so gradually darkening. When the party started, the sun would just be touching the horizon, setting the entry hall ablaze. Lamps would be lit in the courtyards, and the jewels on the ladies stepping out of their carriages would flare in the setting sun. By the time I'd made my entrance, however, the rising moon would have replaced the dying sunlight, emphasizing my midnight dress. I would walk down the main staircase, all those below in the entry hall would look up, and the evening of my dreams would begin.

"There we go," I heard the maid's voice say behind me, and I realized the tugging had stopped. I turned slowly, aware of the weight I carried, and stepped in front of the mirror. The dress looked beautiful; I looked beautiful. The dress fit like I'd been wearing it all my life, yet it emphasized me in ways I had never noticed. The sheer fabric that grew out of the bodice and looped casually around my shoulders did not hide so much as show off my pale skin, and the jewels lent radiance to my slightly flushed face. I didn't look like a nervous child. I looked like the woman I had envisioned in my head in all of my fantasies about this day. I smiled, truthfully this time. I was ready.

I spotted Giselle in the crowd as I made my descent down the staircase; with a straight back, head held high, and a gracious smile on my face. She looked beautiful in a stunning green silk dress that matched her eyes perfectly, her smooth black hair swept back from her head like folded wings. As I made my way to her through the throng, I nodded and smiled at those I passed, recognizing faces from mother's parties. The general air was one of acceptance and encouragement, and I took heart in this feeling as I finally reached Giselle. She drew me into a light, but warm, embrace as we kissed each other's cheeks.

"You look stunning, Evelyn," she said, looking over my outfit. "The star of the ball. Perhaps even more lovely than myself."

"Is that why you've chosen such a jealous shade of dress?" I jested with her, referring to her green attire. She took it in stride, batting her emerald eyes, and we laughed. "It is in fun, Giselle. You look simply wonderful."

"I wouldn't want to outshine my sister, though," she said. "It is your night, after all." We began to walk through the mingling crowd, arms linked. "Quite a turn out, sister," she said softly. "And they all look quite impressed with you."

"I hope they are impressed with the party as well," I said.

"Let us go into the ballroom then, and see what entertainment has been provided," my sister said, and we turned through the giant open double doors.

It was everything I had hoped for. The usual golden glow of the ballroom had miraculously turned to silver. The tapers on the walls had been coated silver and the sconces dripped with crystals that looked like icicles. The red curtains had been exchanged for dark blue ones; the velvet was only shades lighter than my dress. The musician's stand in the far corner was draped in a silver canopy, and the musicians themselves all wore navy blue uniforms with silver braiding. The full moon shining through the many tall windows cast the room in a shimmering light, and as I passed by one of the mirrored panels on the wall, I saw it playing off the nearly hidden jewels in my corset and giving the dress a slight halo. Those gathered around the edges of the ballroom and in the hall behind me sighed, and I felt a blush work itself up into my cheeks.

In the center of the ballroom stood my mother and father, watching my approach. I felt Giselle drop my arm and fall a few steps behind me as I moved toward my parents. Mother wore a rich violet gown, the color of deepest shadows, a string of pearls and opals around her neck. Father stood beside her in a black suit, accented with silver embroidery, and a cummerbund the same color as mother's gown. Her gloved hand was laid on father's arm lightly, but I could see their fingers intertwined.

I curtsied before them. My father bowed his head, and mother reached out to me. I put my hand in hers and stood between my parents.

"Honored guests," my father spoke in a voice that carried to the edges of the room, "may we present to you our second eldest daughter, Evelyn, on the eve of her sixteenth year." The room resounded with applause, and I smiled, blushing once more. I felt my mother's hand squeeze mine tightly. "Supper is waiting in the dining room," my father continued, "and afterwards we shall work it off with some dancing." Warm laughter flowed through the room, and I took my father's arm with pride, marveling at his apparently effortless charisma, as he escorted me across the parquet.

I was both honored and comforted by his strong presence as he led me down the long dinner table and stood with me at the head while everyone else filled in behind Giselle and mother. Livered servants pulled out the guests' chairs, while our father sat me first at the right of the table in the place of honor, then Giselle and finally our mother, before sitting down himself at the head of the table. The guests were seated, the linen napkins were placed, and silver platters began streaming out of the kitchen doors onto the table.

As our plates were filled, I experimentally took a sip of my wine. It was rich and fruity, and very strong. I suppressed a cough, swirling the goblet as I'd seen my mother do. I had never had spirits before, but it did not taste unpleasant, and I took another drink, letting the wine sit on my tongue a moment before swallowing.

"How do you find the wine, Evelyn?" I heard my father say, and I looked up into his dark eyes.

"It is new to me," I said slowly, testing the words in my mind before speaking. "It is quite strong, but the aroma is appealing."

"It is a red wine from my personal vault," he said, lifting his own glass. "On the day of your birth, a single cask of this wine arrived in a shipment. The captain said he'd had to trade nearly half the cargo for this single crate, but assured me it was worth it, that the one sip he'd had revealed its worth. I have saved it these sixteen years for this evening." The servants withdrew, and my father stood, glass in hand. "A toast then, to Evelyn," he said, and everyone's glass was lifted into the air. "May this evening be the beginning of many wonderful years to come, and may she find all that she seeks in this world."

"To Evelyn," Giselle said, "that she may experience all that life has to offer."

"To Evelyn," my mother said, "that she may always follow her heart."

"To Evelyn," the guests chorused, and I took my third sip of the wine of my birth.

In no time at all, we were re-entering the ballroom. The moon had risen higher in our absence, now hanging like a luminous pendant in the sky. The band had already started with a simple, introductory song. People had paired off and were approaching the musician's tent where a courageous few had already begun promenading around the dance floor. At the head of the dancers I recognized Giselle in the arms of the Count of Viscarrie, who had called several times the past year for an audience with the eldest daughter of the house. He was a handsome man of some thirty years, already experienced in sorcery and the politics of court life. People near his tower spoke of giant storm heads in the shape of chimeras, raining down hail the size of crystal balls and lightning bolts that would chase down the street in jagged flashing blazes before careening back into the sky. He was well known in many neighboring kingdoms, and was rumored to be a distant prince himself. Giselle had begun courting him in earnest more than a year ago, when she was making a return from a party with Mother and myself. It was the small hours of the morning, and the man-made thunder and lightning put us all on edge. Finally, Giselle could take it no longer. She jumped from the carriage, stalked up the long drive to his tower, boldly knocked on his front door, and bid him stop the dreadful quaking, it was giving her an appalling headache. And before anyone knew it, the count had presented himself before her father, to begin the expected year of courtship before asking for Giselle's hand in marriage. From then on, those near the tower reported the same dazzling spectacles, but completely void of sound.

A betrothal was imminent, but I was glad that Giselle had waited until after my special night to enact it. She caught my eye as she twirled past and I inclined my head to her, thankful that she had made sure that the dancing had begun without the awkward moment of who would be first on the floor. She winked and danced away.

I made my way around the floor, speaking with those who stood on the sidelines, thanking them for coming and making sure that all their needs had been taken care of. Mother had properly coached me, making sure I knew that this party was more for my guests than it was for me. As hostess, it was up to me to make sure the party progressed smoothly, and that my distinguished guests found my skills and charm acceptable.

As I continued to greet, I began to notice a pattern among my guests. As I greeted the man and wife of each house, the wife would soon begin to talk about her son, or sons if she was so blessed, and impress upon his many good qualities, or produce the lad himself, barely containing her enthusiasm as she pushed him at me. I kept a polite face with all these potential prospects. Mother had warned me about these women, who would take no time to shove their sons in my face in hopes that I would be surprised into revealing my interest or favor, which they would latch onto in the months to come. I should politely inquire about their health, if they were enjoying themselves, and then make my farewells to the family and move onto the next guest. The idea was to give every family equal time so as not to show favoritism, while letting each one know that I was interested and open to possibilities. As I finished my round and came up beside my mother, the small smile she gave me let me know that I had done well.

"How are you doing, my Evelyn?" she asked as she looped her arm through mine.

"Very well, Mother, thank you," I said. She smiled at my carefully held composure, and I couldn't repress a grin. "It is beyond all my wildest dreams," I said truthfully, hugging her arm tightly to my side. She kissed my forehead, then daintily pinched my nose, and we both laughed.

"What are you two finding so amusing?" Giselle's voice threaded through the hum of voices and violins, and we turned to see her walking towards us. We both held our arms out to her, and she clasped our hands, beaming. "Well, I think the evening has gotten off to a fabulous start," she said in an appraising tone.

"Start?" I echoed. "But the party has been going on for hours."

"Little Evelyn," my sister said patronizingly, shaking her head with a knowing smile, "the party has just begun."

It was on my second tour of the ballroom an hour later that I saw him. I did not know how I had missed him before; I was sure that I had spoken to everyone. But as I stood near the windows striking conversation, a reflection in the perfectly polished glass caught my eye, and I found myself entranced by it, though I could make out no more than a chiseled profile, wavy hair and a pale suit. I excused myself as quickly as I could without offending my company and strode around the perimeter of the dance floor sedately, but keeping a sharp eye on my target. His back was to me now, the long suit jacket trimmed with white embroidery, hands clasped behind him as he stood listening to the musicians. His curly blonde hair was pulled back into a queue at the nape of his neck. I found myself noticing little details about his appearance: the apparent ease of his strong stance, the slight tilt of his head to the left as though processing the notes he heard, and the absence of a band on his fourth finger.

As I drew near, he turned around to face me, an easy smile on his face. I began to sink into a curtsey, but he held up his hand. "Please, the pleasure is all mine, mademoiselle," he said in a voice that seemed on the verge of laughter. He clicked his heels together and made a respectful bow, taking hold of the hand I extended him and barely brushing his lips against it. Yet that faint touch sent a deep shiver through my core.

"I must apologize, good sir," I said, collecting myself. "I confess that while talking to my guests, I appear to have overlooked you."

"It's not your fault," he said, his voice still happy and light. "I am easy to overlook tonight, especially when your beauty outshines the very stars."

It took all my concentration not to give into the deep blush threatening behind my cheeks. "You are too kind, sir," I demurely replied, inwardly thrilled by his words.

"Not at all," he insisted. "Allow me to introduce myself. I'm Charles Mercer. And you must be the lovely Miss Evelyn Cavanaugh."

"Indeed I am, sir."

"That is good, for you are too beautiful to not be the focus of tonight's party."

Despite my teachings to keep thoughts hidden and emotions composed, his handsome face and winning words put a smile on my lips. I was unaccustomed to such effective flattery, and his compliments affected me far more than the contrived ones of my other guests.

He gazed at me with bright merry eyes. "Would you care to dance?" he asked, now extending his hand to me, a hopeful smile on his face.

Thoughts ran through my head in rapid succession. Charles Mercer was perhaps the most gorgeous man I had ever seen, certainly at this party. He was witty, charming and gracious, and I found myself wishing to respond to his advances. I could not banish the feeling of his lips on my hand.

However, I had never seen this man before, or his family. The name Mercer was unfamiliar to me. I knew practically nothing about him, besides his name, good looks and charming personality. I had been advised not to show favor to any particular gentlemen, not without confirmation from my mother that is was fine to proceed.

But I found that I didn't care for propriety at the moment. This moment in time was mine to experience. This was the secret reason behind my debut, to meet a handsome man who could sweep me off my feet, as mother had met father all those years ago. And I knew, that no matter the outcome of this evening, or of my life, I would have this wonderful moment to remember.

So I put my hand in his. "I would love to," I said.

It was like all the dreams I'd had since I had first learned about my debut had erupted out of my head and descended upon my surroundings in shining splendor. I whirled around the ballroom in the long arms of Charles Mercer to the stirring of strings and lilting flutes. The moon, now high in the night sky, illuminated the parquet under the feet of the dancers till it shone like water. I had glimpsed Giselle as the dance had led us around the room. The emotions on her face went from big-eyed shock, to a little worried frown, then smoothing into a lovely smile before I was whirled away.

I looked up into my partner's face often, and he was always looking down at me, a smile on his face that threatened to melt my composure. He was never less than gentlemanly though, and even when the dance got more complex, his hand and foot was always carefully placed. It was hard to keep my guard around him though. His merry face invited me to throw off my inhibitions and forget myself, even though my guests and family surrounded us.

As the music began to grow into the final crescendo, we slowly stopped on the edge of the floor by the entrance hall, unaware of the frenzy of dancers around us. His hands found mine, and I could feel several pairs of eyes upon us. I wondered how we looked to them, he in his pale grey suit like the moon, to my dress and its starry splendor. The moment was perfect, and my face was already raised and waiting expectantly when he inclined his head down. I read in his face the unspoken question, and closed my eyes in answer.

In doing so, I failed to see the arrival of my younger sister.

The music faded into silence, but it wasn't till I felt Charles let go of my hands that I knew that something had changed. Whatever the evening had been leading up to was gone, and now something else, something just as important to my future, and me, was occurring. I opened my eyes, and nearly closed them again. A bright light, intensified by the shimmering darkness my eyes had become accustomed to, shone from the entrance into the ballroom. I squinted my eyes as the golden beams faded to a soft glow, and then my eyes opened wide as my spine stiffened in shock.

Rose stood in the arched doorway, the very image of loveliness. The woman I had seen in the mirror before the party couldn't hold a candle to my sister, even with my added advantage of three years. Rose's beauty went beyond age to something timeless. Her hair, hanging long and loose, looked more carefully created than my own coiffeur. She was dressed in a gown of pinks and gold, enhancing her golden hair and rosy cheeks. The dress looked like it had grown in petals around her been adorned with a sunbeam. The darkened ballroom should have swallowed her, but her blue eyes shone with such beauty that she overpowered the deepest shadows. Standing before her, I felt like the moon being outshined by the sun, the sparkling diamonds in my dress now as dim as fading stars before the dawn.

As I looked on, I saw my parents a little ways from me, walking towards Rose. My mother stood before her, hands reaching uncertainly, as though she feared her youngest daughter would run. But Rose remained there, and my mother bent to kiss the top of her head. I understood my mother's conflicting interests, how it was my party, my evening, and yet how Rose had never before shown any interest in showing herself in the public eye, had never acquiesced to our mother's wishes. She suddenly looked back towards the crowd, but it took her a moment to locate me, dark in the shadows of the moonlit ballroom. When her eyes found me, I could see the private struggle on her face.

Meanwhile, my father had leaned down to Rose, and I could see him saying something to her. She nodded, and he offered her his arm. My mother turned back to them, and quickly walked over, whispering something urgent in my father's ear. A look of confusion passed across his face, but it quickly cleared, and he turned Rose around, leading her back to the staircase instead of into the ballroom. The players shook the dazed look from their eyes and grabbed their forgotten instruments, startling me with loud abrupt opening notes, and I shook my head as though I was waking from a dream. The moon still shone in the night sky, the guests still mingled, talked and danced. It was as though nothing had changed. But everything had. The talk had become quiet. The dancers that passed by the entrance craned their heads as they spun, looking towards the staircase. I could feel eyes on me, yet when I looked at others, they turned away. I finally turned to look at Charles, hoping that he would still be looking at me in that wonderful way, like I was the only woman in the room.

But of course, I wasn't. Even though Rose had left, her memory eclipsed me. Charles was still looking towards the staircase, his mouth slightly open. When he finally did turn to me, I knew he didn't see me. "Who was that?" he gasped without preamble.

My face resumed its well-groomed mask. "That was my younger sister, Rosalind. If you'll excuse me," I said, and walked away without waiting for a response that wasn't coming.

I continued to play the gracious hostess, despite the fact that none would meet my eyes, and my relief did not show as my guests began to leave. I thanked each for coming and weathered their insincere flatteries. One of the last to leave was Charles Mercer. He had that winning smile back in place. "It was a pleasure to meet you, Miss Evelyn," he said warmly.

I managed a polite smile. "And you, Mr. Mercer," I replied, inclining my head briefly, refusing to curtsey. But he refused to be put off, and bowed, taking my hand and pressing his lips to it. I'm sure he intended it to be warm and promising, but it felt as cold and distant as the fading stars. And as he lifted his head to look at me, his eyes rested not on me, but on the grand staircase where my sister had appeared hours ago.

I turned to the last of the departing guests, and finally made my way back through the entryway, the large double doors closing behind me. Inside the ballroom, the servants were efficiently cleansing the remains of the party. Lost gloves, champagne glasses, swatches of fabric and buttons were gathered; the blue curtains were being wrestled down from the windows; musicians were loosening their stiff collars and packing up their instruments. One lone cellist still played, the slowly moving bow releasing long tender notes from the instrument. I stood in the hallway, listening to the melody. Earlier that evening, I would have thought it romantic, a song that I would have danced to with my newly found gentleman. Now, it just sounded achingly sad. I turned from the sight of my dismantled evening and walked up the stairs slowly. My hand trailed on the banister, feeling the smooth wood and nearly invisible joints connecting the great beams of oak. Years of training prevented me from ascending with any less dignity than when I had descended earlier this evening, but I wished I could let my spine curl forward and bow my head from weariness and dejection.

My debut, my first foray into society, had failed. The years of training and planning and yearning were for naught, for no one would remember it was I who had done it. I had heard the whispers, seen the glances. Even now, they were whispering to family and friends of the youngest Cavanaugh sister, the reclusive Rosalind whose beauty rivaled the dawn, who outshone her sister like the sun outshining the moon.

I had instinctively aligned myself to Giselle, my elder, over our share interests and temperaments. Dresses, parties, courtship, society – none of them appealed to Rose, whose greatest joy was reading. She had declined every time our mother had asked her to come to a function. Why had she chosen this night, of all nights, to attend a party? Didn't she know how much this evening had meant to me?

Of course she'd known. I'd talked of nothing else for weeks, months. She had seen how important this was to me, and she destroyed it so effectively, and by doing so little. A little flame of anger bloomed in my head, and I selfishly nurtured it as I reached the top of the stairs and walked past Giselle's room, door already closed. My door stood beside hers, firelight warmly inviting me in, but I turned to look across the hall at Rose's room. The door was ajar, and I could see her, sitting on the cushioned windowsill, head resting against the glass. Her eyes were closed, her breathing deep, yet even in sleep she had a grace I would never possess. I wanted to hate her. I wanted to throw open her door and stride in screaming, let her know how much she had wounded me. My anger flared brighter.

But she sighed, and shifted, and the moonlight caught the wet tear trails shining on her face. I looked at her a moment longer, a sudden thought creeping into my head that I would go in, guide her to bed, tuck in the sheets around her. She looked so young.

The moment passed, and I did not enter her room, either in anger or in compassion, but ran downstairs, out the back door, through the gardens and down to the Wood.

There are two paths that circle the Wood that backs our city and spreads through the center of our land. Birch and poplar trees line one path, the straight path, an arrow in the sparse undergrowth. Devoid of sprawling roots that can twist an ankle, and with no wild ivy encroaching on the sides, the traveler can always see the magnificent houses and lights of the city beyond the Wood's edge. My father likes us to take this path. He says the other path is too dangerous for young ladies such as ourselves. Giselle agrees and walks primly, a little puff of dust emphasizing her steps. Rose doesn't walk in the Wood at all, preferring to run through the grassy pastures at its edge. When we are together, I walk behind, head inclined, eyes lowered as I've been taught.

Yet I have always wondered about the other path. I've often imagined the enormous redwoods, the ferns and creepers, and the silence, not even bird song. They say there has been no sign of any animal living in the Wood for many years. When I first heard of the strangeness of the Wood, I approached my father, to see if he could provide me with an explanation. But he would not tell me anything further, only that I should stay on the brightly lit path, the safe one.

But I do not always do as he says.

At night, the Wood looked larger, wilder, very unlike the vague swath of green I saw daily from our house's windows. But I was driven by a desperate need to be away, away from my family, away from my sixteenth year, away from my life. I couldn't remember ever before being unhappy with the world around me, but now it felt stifling, strangling. I passed by the first path, and plunged deep into the undergrowth.

Intruder.
Wake up, ready to attack.
Grass, trees, moon above.
Listen. Nothing.

Feels like ice cracking on river.
Something here.
Run.
Fight.

The trees stood at attention, as I watched every step, wary of roots placed in just the right place to trip the unwary. Everything looked as though it were underwater; even the air around seemed to ripple with every step. I brushed trailing creepers away as I rushed by, but nearly falling over a root as thick as my forearm made me pause. My anger, pain, sadness died in my throat, and was replaced by a small cold fear. With all the thick trees, low branches and creeping ferns, it took me more than a few moments to locate the path. Thankfully, though nearly hidden, it was there. At least I was not lost. But I was alone, my solidarity amplified by the unnatural quiet surrounding me. I remained still, fingers curled into my palms of their own accord, straining for a sound.

And then, finally, I did hear something. Not animal, but a low rushing. I turned my eyes downward, keeping the path in sight as I navigated my way through the wispy ferns.

River loud.
Getting close.
Climb tree to watch, wait.
Nothing.
Wait.

Though I tried to keep my thoughts on not getting lost, my fantastic surroundings kept drawing my gaze. I had never seen trees so thick and twisted, unlike the pale straight birches of the first path. The branches seemed to go on forever in every direction, weaving a blanket of bark and darkness above my head. I pick a branch at random to follow, and it took me nearly four-dozen steps to get to the end of it. I lowered my head, hand rubbing the newly formed crick in my neck, and froze. As I had feared, I had lost the path.

After silently berating myself for being distracted so easily, I listened for the sound, the low whisper, an audible trail to follow. I raised my dress up as I picked my way over weathered grey stones, and felt something catch the hem of my dress, my beautiful dress. I remembered what was behind me, and my anger returned as I stomped through the underbrush, hands clenched. Then I cleared the last of the trees, and the sight before me erased all thoughts of frustration or home.

A girl?
Almost fall.
Long hair. Smile. Happiness. Human.
Why?

The only time I had ever seen this much water was at the lake my family visited every summer, but this moving mass of water was so different. The lake had been still, a glass mirror, but this was molten, moving and rolling and so alive. My feet flew of their own accord to the edge of the water, and I knelt down, feeling the faint spray and droplets land on my face and hands. I felt the anger fading out of my cheeks.

Kneels down.
Hand touches water – and a jolt shudders through my spine, crashes in my skull. A thousand thoughts, a thousand questions, fill my mind. I can't see straight. What is her name, why is she here, what does she smell like, what color are her eyes as she stares out at the river before her like a rippling carpet? I try to focus as she shimmers like the night sky. She is beautiful. How long has it been since I'd appreciated a maiden's beauty, complemented a woman's face?

As I let the water drip off my hands, enjoying the whispering sounds the river made and the dappled moonlight shining through the leaves, I wondered why no one else took the path that led out here. Though it was more twisted and treacherous than the straight birch-lined trail at the edge of the Wood, it could easily be navigated if you paid attention.

Besides, it was beautiful out here, a picturesque scene made silver in the moonlight. The grass cushioned my footsteps, and I wondered how it would feel on my bare feet, like string, or curls of paper, perhaps.

The thought made me pause, one foot hovering, and I looked at it, wondering. There was no one out here. I'd just see for one moment whether it did feel like that. Then I'd continue on, and no one would know of my slip of decorum. I looked around, expecting to see people peeking out from behind the trees, then caught myself and laughed. Leaning against a low-hanging branch, I slid one bare foot out and stepped onto the grass.

It was unlike anything I'd felt before, soft like fur, but springy too. I wiggled my toes and laughed again. If anyone had seen me like this, I would have been mortified, but I was alone and could be giddy without fear. I kicked the other shoe off and took a few cautious steps, then a few more, and then I was off, spinning around in a blur, all decorum forgotten. This is how the evening had felt in the beginning – all the silver and blue, the excitement and joy, and now, the only audience was the trees around me.

She looks so happy, so carefree, hair in her face, feet skimming the ground, the jewels in her dress leaving streaks in the air like shooting stars. I want to run, to join her. My legs twitch at the thought, but I'm tampered by a glance at the river, seemingly harmless, yet a fence more solid than iron and as powerful as lightning. Blurry memories of previous attempts to cross it make me wince in pain.

She stops, and her face suddenly sharpens before me, exhilarated yet aching. Her eyes are wet. She's frozen, a deer in the undergrowth. And then she blurs into movement, finds her shoes, smoothes her hair, wipes her tears, and suddenly, she is gone. My mind starts to slip, and I remember her face, bathed in shades of gray and moonlight, stunning as a star – *silence.*

Jump down.

Grass, river, moon above. Nothing.

- just a dream -

Stomach tight, hunger.

Hunt.

I don't remember how I got back home that night, only that I awoke the next morning with my feet coated in blades of grass.

- THREE -

EXILE

My debut marked the beginning of the end for our family as we once were. Father's ships started arriving in port nearly destroyed by stormy rapids, ransacked by pirates, or disappearing all together. Civil wars slowed the caravan trading to a crawl. Father had gotten the company through such situations before, it was all part of his work. But then, Mother got sick, too quickly and too intensely. The constant stream of doctors that Father hired all said the same. There was nothing to be done. Giselle, Rose and I sat with Mother for most of our days, doing needlepoint together, practicing our music, or listening to Rose read aloud to us. Sad as it was, it was one of the few times I could remember the women of my family so close, mother and daughters happy in each other's company. Mother never seemed in any pain, but it seemed to me she grew a little dimmer every day. My mother, once the light of the city, no longer received visitors. Instead she wrote letters to her friends, often short because she couldn't keep her hand steady for long. Rose offered to write for her, but Mother waved her offer away, still proud as she had always been. Whenever Father came home, they would sequester themselves off in their room, leaving us daughters like drifting boats without an anchor, wandering from room to room until we could excuse ourselves to bed.

I never saw her weak, not even the day she died. We were sitting around her bed, listening to Rose read a poem about grapes filled with sun and the taste of summer, when she suddenly held up a hand and said to Giselle, "Will you please send for your father?" She said it so calmly, but Giselle bolted upright and ran out the door. Rose's eyes suddenly flooded with tears, little tremors shaking her body. Trying to keep as calm as Mother, I took one of her hands in my left, and Rose's in my right. Rose took Mother's free hand and we sat there, a silent circle, hoping, praying, for minutes until Father burst in with Giselle in close pursuit. He took in the scene, then said, "Could you please wait outside, girls? I'll be right out." Giselle came over and Mother kissed her on the forehead, then me, then Rose, raising a hand to wipe the tears from her cheeks. We slowly filed out, the door closed, and as one we fell to the floor, legs too weak to stand. We knew before Father came out that it was over, but it still hit me in the gut when he spoke the words we knew were coming. He leaned over and pulled Giselle and me up gently, then gathered Rose in his arms and led us outside to the front porch.

All day we sat there, as doctors and morticians, friends and associates came by in an unending parade of questions and comfort. My first impression of death was that it was very hard work, or at least hard for those it left behind. Father never faltered in his responses, though, and when one or all of us would start to cry again, he would gather us tighter together. But I did not see him cry, not once during that long, beautiful day. Mother's funeral was filled to bursting with the people she had known and touched in her life, but instead of their gay colors and sparkling conversation, they dressed in black and spoke in whispers. Mother would have cried to see her friends so dark and somber.

Father did not leave the house much after that. He remained in the little-used office behind the sitting room, the only sound that of paper rustling and pens scratching. But the business continued to suffer. I entered the sitting room one day to see it completely empty. The furniture, the rugs, wall sconces and paintings, all gone. Outside the office door was a piece of paper, and when I brought it to my sisters, Rose told us that it was a list of all the parts of the sitting room, their total worth, and then that number subtracted from a much larger number. I could tell Giselle knew more about what it meant than I did, but she feigned ignorance and we left the invoice back at Father's door.

The same thing happened the next week to the dining room. Then the parlor, the entrance hall, the grand staircase, and the more of our life that disappeared, the less we saw of Father. I knew he was trying, but the collapse was inevitable. Our neighbors knew we were done for, and moved within days of Mother's funeral. For all of his business sense, Father's empire had thrived and grown through the greatest of luck, and it became increasingly clear his luck had run out. The news of our eventual ruin spread like wildfire. We were avoided like the plague. Bad luck could spread as easily as a cold, and when one of us went outside, the people on the street immediately turned away. Then one day, Father left the little office for good, gathered us together and confirmed our growing fears: there was nothing left of his business. The royal family, having been acquainted with us, was kind enough to pardon the enormous amount of money we owed to all those working for and counting on Father and his business, but they weren't kind enough to let us stay in our beautiful house, in the city. We were to pack only the essentials, and we would be leaving within a week.

I couldn't help it – I burst into tears, ashamed of my weakness but too emotionally exhausted to help myself. Giselle began to cry too, but even in her sadness she looked regal, a queen mourning over the loss of her kingdom. Rose was somber, but her eyes remained dry, and she began to ask Father questions about packing, dates and travel. I listened, numb, as Father detailed how we were to go through our things, leave behind our jewels, ball gowns, shoes, hair combs, anything of value to be sold.

"But, what will we wear in our new home?" Giselle asked, indignant. "We'll need our things to cement our standing."

Father looked pained, and a gnawing feeling began deep in my stomach. "Giselle," he said, "we won't need them where we're going."

"Nonsense, even though the neighboring cities are smaller, they still have the same rules. We are still Cavanaughs."

"We're not moving to another city, Giselle."

"Then where?"

He was silent, and I waited for the inevitable blow. "We are moving to Magnasaltus. It is a village in the lumber district, about a months travel from here. It is far enough away that no one will bother us, or know who we are."

I had never even heard of the name Magnasaltus, and I feared it was not from a lack of geographical knowledge, but because it was so small it didn't matter enough to be placed on a map. Giselle drew in a sharp breath. "But a village…that's little more than a mess of houses. There will be no society in a village. Why would we live there?"

But he remained silent, and it was then that I began to realize just how far we had fallen.

Giselle continued loudly, almost a scream. "The Count of Viscarrie will not be seen with a village-dweller, much less court one. We must be married, immediately. He would help, if you would let him, I doubt he'd refuse his fiancée anything. I'll send word to him immediately!"

"The Count is no longer an option, Giselle."

"Why ever not?"

"Giselle, we're not part of the elite anymore," said Rose quietly. Giselle, stunned, turned to Father, eager for him to counter Rose's words, but he did not. "I am so sorry, my dears," he said quietly, unable to meet our gazes. I barely noticed Giselle swiftly exit the room, but after hours had passed without her return, I saddled our second to last horse and rode to the tower in the gathering twilight to find our last horse tied to the gate at the bottom of the Count's long drive, along with several people who all turned away from me and hurried along their way without a word. Giselle was standing at his door, her fists clenched, bruised and cracked from hammering at his door for hours, and even now, the fierce gaze she trained on the wood seemed enough to reduce it to splinters. I had to gently lead her away, back to the horse and home in the soft night, punctuated only by silent stares and swift movements from those we passed on the street, anxious to be as far from us as they could, but wanting every sordid detail of our journey.

Our possessions were stripped from us, our past lives were carted off day after day, until only the house was left, which wouldn't get a cent. We knew the moment we moved out, our lovely mansion would be burned down. Bad times didn't belong in the city. That was for the smaller towns and villages, where we were destined. When the dawn of our departure arrived, clear and cold, we packed our own wagon that would join with the caravan train at the gate leading out of the city. Giselle stood stoic at the doorway, looking down the road, her hands wrapped in linens and gauze, waiting for a miracle, salvation from the inevitable. Rose struggled to load her luggage, and when I reached down to lift it, I could hear the rustle of hundreds of papers. After she went back in the house, I looked inside to see dozens and dozens of books, some thinner than slate, others encased in stiff velveteen covers, all bearing battered corners and worn spines. I considered confronting her. Surely Father would have rather sold these than haul their dead weight with us. Instead, I pushed the box to the corner and covered it with a blanket. I went up to Giselle, and took her bandaged hand, small comfort that it was, and drew her up into the back of the wagon. Her eyes remained fixed behind us, refusing to blink through her tears until what had been our house disappeared into the midst of the receding city. It wasn't until that night, when we were trying to sleep on our most comfortable possessions in the wagon, the entire caravan train halted on the edge of the nearest town, that I asked Rose about the books.

"I was going to get rid of them. I didn't want to, but I thought it best. But when Father saw me stacking them to sell, he told me to keep my oldest ones, that they wouldn't be worth selling. I think he was trying to be nice, in his own way."

"That does sound like Father," I said, keeping my envy tightly bound. Who was I to wish Rose an unsure future without even her beloved books at her side? If there were something I loved as much as Rose loved her books, I would have done all I could to take it with me too. As it was, my lack of worldly possessions was unnerving. "Rose," I ventured, "do you think I could... read one of your books? I haven't read much since we learned our letters as children, and it would be nice to have something to do on our journey."

"Of course," said Rose, and it may have been a trick of the moonlight sneaking through the curtains of the wagon, but I thought I saw both a smile and tears on her face.

It only took twenty-seven days to make the journey, but it may as well have been twenty-seven years. With the city far behind us, every town we passed diminished in size until we seemed to be completely surrounded by wilderness, with only the Wood to guide us. I tried to be thankful for the caravans, jostled and jolted as we were by every bump in the road, which made travel safer and more convenient for reading. We quickly dove into the books Rose had smuggled aboard, records of historical places and figures, chronicles of neighboring countries and guides of flora and fauna. Rose devoured knowledge voraciously. Even in these reread tomes, she often shared new facts with me she had missed in past viewings. I didn't find them nearly so fascinating. True, these books greatly improved my previous reading skills, but I couldn't continue the same book for more than a day without growing weary of it. One particularly stifling afternoon, after struggling through a very elaborate breakdown of the common bumblebee's anatomical systems, I threw the book back with the others, caring very little if it got hurt in the process.

Rose looked up from her book with a pained expression. "No need to take your frustrations out on the books," she chastised. "If you don't understand a word, just ask me."

"It's not that again," I said, rubbing the bridge of my nose. "I know these pages are your pride and joy, but I just cannot seem to get invested in the cross-species pollinations of orchids and snap trap plants like you do."

"You should, it's fascinating," she said. "Imagine, flowers that could fight back. But here, why don't you try my book about the shipping industry?"

"I did, days ago, and I don't think my views on the import lists of various cities over the past decade has changed since then." I looked out the back of the caravan at the horizon, seemingly unchanged since dawn. "Maybe this was a foolish cause. I'm not like you. I'm more fit for dances and gossip than the goings-on of the world."

"That's not true," Rose said sharply, and I turned back to see her snap her book shut and wag it in my face. "I'm so tired of people saying they can't do one thing or another. Books are freedom, thought and thinking and being more. You are too made for more." Seemingly spent, she gestured with her book to the box. "You just have to find one that...talks to you."

"They all do a great deal of talking at me," I muttered.

"Not at you, *to you*. Find one that talks to you, and makes you want to talk back, learn more." She reopened her book. "And fix the one you threw in there."

With not an undue amount of grumbling, I leaned over the crate and picked up the naturalistic book, splayed, but not bent. Underneath, a shimmer of silver caught my eye. I reached down to feel soft velvet and cold foil, and emerged with a book I hadn't yet seen. Small, no bigger than my hand, but surprisingly thick, the book had a cover embroidered with silver thread. It depicted a series of rolling hills, not unlike the ones we traveled, with a large bird flying above. It was titled simply *On and On*.

Wary, but curious, I sat back with it and opened to the first page.

Contained within these pages, a collection of stories, writ to delight, to inspire, to terrify, to dare, to dream.

What followed was story after story, tales of heroism and barbarity, quests and imprisonment, love and miracles. When I finally raised my head, it was to discover night had fallen. Rose slept soundly across the caravan, but had left behind a plate of food at my elbow and a precious candle, which had been lit without my realizing it, and provided the light I needed to keep reading. I ate quickly and blew out the candle, but as I lay in bed, with only starlight to see by, I ran my fingers over the cover again and again, as though I could absorb new stories into my blood.

The following days seemed brighter. Now I was the one who shared what she read, and Rose would tell me what region the story had come from, what common themes it shared with other tales, the symbolism of a certain character or animal. The book, she explained, was from her childhood, given and often read to her by Mother. Upon learning of the book's origins, I thought she would be jealous of my viewing such an intimate thing, but rather, she seemed excited by my continued reading. Maybe it was because I had proven her right, or because it kept our conversations centered on a safe topic in the midst of our upheaval and exile. It definitely made the days pass faster, for it was in the middle of a story about a boy who has to travel across a desert to save a captured princess that we finally arrived in Magnasaltus.

I was surprised to see so much similarity. Magnasaltus was just as loud, as busy and as colorful as the city, and if the shops were slightly more pragmatic, leaning away from ribbons and toys and more towards bakeries and butchers, they were just as busy. Giselle's expression left no doubt she thought she had arrived in an uncultured wasteland, while Rose had a more cautious optimistic look, like my own. They seemed friendly enough, men doffing hats as we passed through the square, small children scampering the length of the caravans. The shops and buildings began to thin, and minutes later we passed by homesteads nestled in the hills. Cows and sheep gazed dully at us through fence slats as we wove around farmhouses and fields. After a while, even these thinned out, and we meandered back towards the Wood. Rows of birch and poplar trees lined the edge, and I was suddenly struck by the thought that it looked near identical to the path behind our house in the city, the path we were always supposed to take. I began to wonder if that meant there is another second path here, too, but then we turned a corner, and arrived at our new home.

As little as I expected, I was still taken aback. Rose bounded out the back before I could gather myself, and then Father walked inside with her, leaving Giselle and I to help each other down to stare at the structure before us. Small, so small, and erected in unvarnished wooden beams and rough hewn stones. A thick wall of dirt surrounded the entire base of the house, making it look like the structure was sinking. We helped each other to the front door, moving slowly, hoping it would soften the blow of each new discovery. It was dim inside, light turning heavy through the warped windows and descending the rooms into murky darkness. One thin staircase led upstairs, where I could make out two doors, and on the main floor, a living room, a kitchen, and one more door. There was nothing else but the dirt and cobwebs.

Father stood inside by the staircase, silent. We walked up to him, trying to make out the words screaming in our heads. He turned to us, guilt evident in his dejected expression. We all three breathed deep, ready to speak. And then Rose came running out of one of the upstairs doors.

"I've picked my room! It's so lovely, a beautiful window looking out over the hills, and even has a little bit of shelves for my books." She flew downstairs and halted at the kitchen door.

"Well look, we have two fireplaces!" she exclaimed, skipping back through the living room. "We'll be warm in winter, no question. And there's a room back here Father, all for you, go see how big it is! Nearly as large as the kitchen. And did you see the wild ivy growing over the door, just like a picture in a storybook. Oh Father," she sighed, running to him and taking his hands in hers, "it is a lovely house you've found for us."

And just like that, the shame on his face melted away into a supportive smile. "I am so glad you approve, Rose. I think we shall be just fine here." He pulled her into a hug, and I felt my heart sink. It didn't matter what arguments we made. If Rose approved, so did my father. Thanks to her, he viewed this house as an acceptable replacement for the life we left behind. This didn't stop us from loudly voicing how we could not live in this place, but we were now the bad daughters who couldn't be optimistic and grateful like good little Rose. We ran upstairs to the room at the end of the hall and sunk down with our backs against the closed door, tears streaming down our faces as we stared at the empty room that was now ours.

Of course, as the days wore on, we came out of our rooms, helped organize what little furniture we had around the house, began our first forays into the kitchen and discovered what had to be done each day to make the house run. It was here that I really took strides, for Giselle often escaped to her room, and Rose often escaped to our father, so it was up to me to keep the gears turning. Father set aside a monthly allowance for food, so early every morning for the first month I would walk to town. I learned all I could about cooking beef, pork and chicken from the butcher when I bought his wares, and at the bakery, after buying a few of his more expensive pastries, the baker showed me basic recipes for dough to bake my own bread. If I wasn't buying, I was asking everyone for advice on cleaning clothes, washing floors, sweeping hearths and stoking fires. While the girls my age were coolly distant, the younger girls, about Rose's age, were an open book of household knowledge, especially when I offered them the expensive pastries in exchange. After that first month, I had a very basic, but thorough, knowledge of the inner working of running a house. While I did not enjoy it, it did fill me with pride to know how integral I was to our new way of life, and how I had achieved it all on my own determination.

Our house is no longer made of marble and copper, but stone and timber do just as well in keeping the cold out and the warmth in, if not better. The floor is still bare, but it is spotless. The warped glass windows make the scenery outside melt and run together like a watercolor, but they are thick and well sealed, the only luxury the house offers. The only sounds we hear are the wind and the rustling of grass and trees. It has begun to have the charm of home, in its own, rustic way. Rosalind even found a way to improve the ugly foundation of dirt around the house by relocating wildflowers and shrubs from the fields around us. Most of them take to their new homes, and now the muddled colors through the windows are full of yellows and pinks. She had even set aside part of the garden for vegetables and herbs, and taken care of them with her own cobbled-together knowledge of cultivation. But it is one thing to say a place looks quaint, and another thing to live in it, to care for and maintain it, to wash it, rub it, scrub it, and clean it, every day. Rosalind is still taken with the rural pleasantries of the place, tending to her makeshift garden, sweeping her broom with carefree abandon as dust swirls in the air, setting off our fathers' sneezing fits. He doesn't complain though; he just smiles as his eyes run, admonishing Giselle and myself, his two eldest daughters, for not having Rose's sunny disposition. We narrow our eyes and but say nothing, knowing better than to argue with his biased view.

It took months to create the best routine to run our house, and luckily for our survival, there was not much in Magnasaltus to distract me. Whenever I thought I'd achieved the perfect system, the house would throw in a leaky roof, an egg shortage, or a blocked chimney. In the first few months, Father would help with these problems, either solve it on his own, or hire someone from town. He even got a good deal on a brood of hens, and built them a solid coop to keep them safe from rain and foxes. But when winter descended, he began to drift, spending hours, days in front of the fireplace. Whatever help Rose had offered fell through as she began to attend to our father, and I had to admit she had been quite helpful those first few months. But I agreed that our father's health was more important. As spring arrived, though, I became less and less convinced that father was ill, at least physically.

Giselle, though not without her own faults, soon became my only outlet for conversation. She was rubbish at chores, but never made life harder for me, and often sat with me as I worked, talking about our old lives, a subject forbidden or forgotten with the rest of the family. Around the kitchen table, we would plan imaginary parties and meals. By the firelight, we would sew little embroidered designs of pearls and feathers into the décolletage of our plain working clothes. And, late into the night, we'd sit in our room and imagine we could hear the sounds of the city in the quiet wind that whistled through the trees.

Even though a year had passed to let me begin to grow accustomed to its smaller stature and fewer rooms, and even to find comfort in its rustic beauty, there was very little privacy to be found there, and even less when Rose was around. One summer day, she was sitting with Father, as usual, doting on his every whim, asking to hear stories of his travels as a younger man. Giselle was most likely up in our small room, sighing another day away. I was at the kitchen table, ablaze in the evening sun, working out a lumpy pile of dough for this week's loaves. I heard my father and Rose laugh, and a little irritation scratched at the base of my skull, tickled by a trail of sweat. I didn't think it was good for Rose to humor our father this way, letting him reminisce and waste away in front of the fireplace. He was not an old man, and had enough schooling and practical training to get any job in the nearby town. What little money we had was quickly disappearing and, without our father taking a job, unlikely to reappear any time soon. I remembered the vital man who had run around the world to provide for his family, and I was sad, almost embarrassed, to see what he had become.

Another laugh rose up from the parlor, and I slammed the dough down hard against the sturdy table. I lifted and smacked, kneading with my shoulders, taking out my frustration as my face grew hot.

"Sister," I heard Rose call to me. "Could you be quieter please? Father can barely hear himself think."

I refused to answer her; she was not in charge of me. I continued to thump the dough.

"Sister?" Rose's voice was louder, and I looked up to see her standing in the doorway. "Did you hear me?"

"I did indeed," I said evenly, peeling the sticky mass from the tabletop.

"Then could you please knead a little softer?"

"I could, if we want lumpy hard bread for breakfast," I said quietly.

"What?"

"I said, 'tis hard to knead bread dough softly," I stated loud enough for her to hear, and threw the dough down. I suppressed a grin as she winced.

"Evelyn, stop it. You don't have to be so loud."

"Don't I? This is how bread is made, which I don't think you know, considering how you've never made any," I jeered, my blood rising.

"That is unfair, sister. You know our father is not in greatest health, and I have been helping him, while you barely speak to him."

"Well, little Rose, it is hard to find time to play nursemaid in between baking bread, preparing breakfast, lunch and dinner, mopping the floors, cleaning the linens, and the other chores of running a household."

"Nevertheless, he is our father, and he has first priority, above all else. And also, you are not head of this household, he is," she added with an air of intelligent superiority that made me clench my teeth.

"Rose, you know as well as I that he is fine in body. He is making himself ill. And if we let him be in charge, this house would be in shambles. You have to stop pandering to him, Rose, and help out with more pressing matters."

"I help out with the most important matter in this house, our father!"

I couldn't help it. The strain of my shoulders and neck, the sun overheating my face and the anger pounding in my temples fueled my lungs and I started shouting, hands flying wildly in the air. "You don't see it, do you Rose, because you're his favorite!"

"Evelyn Cavanaugh." His low voice cut through our screaming, and we turned to look at the back of the armchair. The top of his head was barely visible above the tall chair back. I couldn't see his face, but his voice showed the stern gaze, the stiff jaw. "That is enough. You will stop this screaming at once."

I lowered my head, feeling my cheeks burning. I glanced over at Rose, who looked similarly chastised, even though Father had not spoken at her. Her eyes flicked over to meet mine, and they were gleaming bright.

"Apologize to Rosalind for your outburst," my father's voice echoed from the chair. My head snapped up then, rage rising in my throat. How dare I apologize, when every word I said was true! There was a long strained silence. My father shifted in his chair so that I could see the side of his face, and even from across the room I could see the eyes, clear and sharp, and I knew I would not disrespect or disobey my father's wishes.

"I am sorry, Rose," I said, keeping my voice carefully emotionless. I turned back towards the dough.

"You are forgiven," I heard Rose say softly. My spine stiffened, but I managed to wrap the dough up in a damp cloth and exit the house, carefully closing the door, before letting the rage flood my face as I fled towards the Wood.

The nerve of her! The absolute gall! I hated her superior commands, pretending to know what was best while avoiding any semblance of help or support, and I hated the way she was clearly my father's favorite. The father I had known on my sixteenth birthday, when he had led me into the dining room on his arm and seated me at his right hand, when he had offered me wine from my birth, was a distant and quickly fading memory. I still loved my father, and craved his affection, but had learned after my mother's death not to seek comfort from him. His grief was too great for him to bear alone, and I would not continue to mourn the past. Things were the way they were, and we had to adjust and make the best of it, which Father was steadfastly avoiding.

I took deep breaths trying to subdue my anger. I began focusing on the birch trees, counting them as I passed by, and again I wondered at how the same path that stretched behind our city could be so long as to continue all the way out to Magnasaltus. I wonder if others know of this. I doubt anyone in Magnasaltus does. The people here fear the Wood in a way I've never seen before. Whereas living close to the Wood, as close as our own backyard, was a symbol of power in the city, dominion over nature, out here the houses clustered on hills far away from the trees of the Wood. Ours is considered to be unnaturally close, and no one can remember who lived there before us.

The rhythmic beat of hooves broke my thoughts, and I looked up to see a man on horseback cantor past me on the path, then turn off it, towards our house. I run after him, and I get back to the house in time to see him ride off again. Father stood in the doorway, an open letter in his hands. His face is guarded, and we gather close around him, past arguments forgotten in worry.

"Another ship has come in. The Heron."

"Is it bigger than the others?" asked Giselle.

"The Heron was my most valuable ship. Last I sent it out was to the southern gem mines. There's been no word of it for nearly three years." He continued to stare at the paper in his hand, as if it would reveal more under closer scrutiny.

"You're going, aren't you?" I asked.

"I have to, tomorrow. If there is a chance that the cargo has survived..."

"But your creditors - "

"I have no choice. But this will be the last. I'll be there and back again before they even know I was there. And besides, what have they to gain by locking up a poor old man in debtor's prison?" He attempted a carefree smile, but we all know that it is dangerous to go back to the city that turned us out, and that every other ship of Father's that had made it back to port had done so empty and broken.

Despite our fear, the returned ship gave us a spark of ill-conceived hope. As we helped him pack for his journey, I knew we were all thinking of what we would do if, against all odds, the cargo were found intact. As we gathered around him the next morning before he set out, he attempted a light-hearted tone. "Well my darlings, what rarities and treasures shall I bring you back from my travels?"

Giselle offered a small smile. "Oh, ribbons and rubies and strands of pearls!"

"Oh yes," I continue the joke, "we must be properly attired when we receive our gentleman callers in the foyer," as I grandly gestured inside our dim little house, "so don't forget the silks and lace!" Father smiled back, and turned to Rose. "And what trinket would you like me to bring you back, my darling Rose?"

"Your safe return is all I require," she said quietly.

Giselle emitted an audible scoff. Father ignored this, focused on Rose. "Anything you ask of me, Rose, and I will bring it back to you."

She paused a moment more, and then, "I would like a rose, father, a living one, if it is not too much trouble."

"A rose for Rose? Of course, my dearest," Father exclaimed and kissed her on the head. He embraced us all and started down the path, soon lost from sight. Giselle and I both turned to stare at Rose.

"Why not ask for a hive of hornets?" Giselle said. "Just as much effort, and both prick you with their thorns."

"What do you mean?" Rose asked, stunned by her reaction, but Giselle just gave an exasperated sigh and stormed inside. Rose turned to look at me, but I avoided her gaze and walked inside too.

I had thought Father's absence might encourage camaraderie between us all, with the removal of the obvious favoritism that divided us. But I suppose too much had already transpired to make our relations easy to reform. No day passed without some fight, the rest spent in tense and uncomfortable silence, and it was hard to tell which was worse. We fought about the chores, about the weather, about each other's habits, anything to battle the silence, and the anxiety that arose whenever we thought too hard about what news Father would bring back. Giselle began to dream of life in the city, our former glory and all our friends returned to us as though we'd never left. When she shared these thoughts, Rose would rise to challenge the fairytale she'd created, impossible to attain even if the ship was completely intact with all its treasures. I refused to voice an opinion, but did not try to stop them, focusing on cooking and cleaning. I was never a peacekeeper.

The truth was, what I wanted was beyond hoping for. I didn't want to stay here anymore, but the life I wanted was not waiting for me in the city. My resentment towards Rose, my frustration and loss had hardened inside me and made it impossible to forgive her for what had happened on my debut, even if it was now two years ago in a life we no longer had. In the trip we took from the city, our grief and loss of self had made connection through her books possible. But while grief had bonded us, anger tore us apart. After the third week, I could not even speak to Giselle. We moved through the house like vipers, likely to strike at the slightest provocation, hiding in our dark corners each night as the dying summer winds whipped around the house and flung sheets of rain at our windows. I began to hope for Father's quick return, no matter what news he would bring with him.

Storm coming.
Need fire.
Break branches, easy to carry, stack.
Sshhhiraaahh...Fire.
Not hungry now. Run long.
Run fast.
Run far.
Farther.
Must stop.
Tired, home.
Wait.
Strange smell, horse. Something else.
Grains, fruit, scorched meat.
And...
Man.
Smell, taste in air. Inside my home.
Hear his breathing. Relaxed. Soft. Sleeping.
Stranger. Enemy.
Stalk, ready to pounce, and – there he sleeps, the man who entered my home, ate at my table, warmed himself by my fire. Never has a man come this far into my domain, and I fight between joy and fear. I focus on my surroundings. Food fills the table. I try to focus on where it comes from, as I often have before, to no avail. But these are the same spirits who start my fires, and tried to feed me when I first came. They had served him dinner. I study him, this stranger, this man. I can smell sea salt and the cold wind of the storm on him. A traveler, then. But he looks too old; his thick dark hair is shot with grey, and deep lines traverse his forehead.

I shake my head, moving closer to him, and his hand twitches. I freeze, but he merely shifts in his sleep and grows still once more. I do not know what keeps me from waking him and throwing him out. After the many years of loneliness, perhaps this man, who had eaten my food and now slept in my home, was different. He felt different than any other who had come here. Maybe one of those nearly forgotten human traits had resurfaced, to pity and empathize with this man so far from home. Maybe it was mere curiosity. But whatever it was, it stayed and vanquished any anger I might have felt toward him, this unknown man. The spirits of this place had chosen to help this man, just as they had helped me all the years of my solitude, and I wouldn't go against them, not after they had been my only companions, silent and invisible, but always there. He couldn't stay. He wouldn't stay. He would return home. And I would remain.

I did not sleep. How could I? Every sound I heard made me think he was waking, coming towards me. I was terrified of him, and at the same time wanted to run and wake him, talk with him, as I hadn't with another being in countless years. Who knew how long I would remain in control of my faculties, able to converse and understand more than mere senses could provide? By dawn I still hadn't come to any decision, but I had to know what became of him. I streaked silently through the castle hallways to the gallery above the sitting room, whose columned balcony offered protection from the man's eyes.

It is not hard for me to remain motionless, to crouch low to the ground, to be still as stone as I lay in wait for the unsuspecting prey to cross my path. I couldn't see him, but I saw the empty dining table and the fire, soft and low, the same white as the morning sun that today, of all days, had finally come over the horizon. The spirits still tended the fire. What did they see in this man, and more importantly, what did this man see in them?

My thoughts were interrupted by the sound of a yawn. It sounds so small in my ears, and yet it echoes inside my head. A human yawn, after so many years of whispering shadows and dark silence. I feel the spirits rush in towards the sound, and after a moment, the warm smells of breakfast waft up to me.

And there he is through the doorway, blanket around his shoulders like a cape, swaying sleepily in front of the fire. I can see the relaxation on his face, the softening of his worry lines, the general air of youth he exudes after only one night's sleep here. He sits at the only place set, the table already filled with food.

His eating mesmerizes me. Had I once used fork and knife, cups and pitchers? His portions seem woefully pitiful to me, yet he looks overwhelmed by what has been provided. He takes bites, chews meditatively, looks around the room to appreciate the draperies, uses the linens. When was the last time I'd wiped my mouth with a napkin? It was his hands that truly captivated me, alighting and floating through the air like pale birds.

He sighs deeply after he finishes eating, pushes away from the table and leans back in the chair, face to the ceiling and eyes closed. My mouth starts salivating and, much to my horror, I feel my back legs tense. His exposed neck, and the languidly throbbing pulse residing there, beckon to me, invite me to taste. I am hungry, two days without food, deprived of last night's meal that would have satiated me. This man has unknowingly made himself a target.

Pounce. Swipe. Bite.

I hold my breath, forcing my legs backwards instead of forwards, retreating behind the heavy curtains. The moment I was out of sight, I run for the nearest open window and leap into the trees beyond it. I should have left the moment he appeared. I am a danger to him. The scent of the leaves rushing by my face does little to mask the smell of that man. I can still recall it, meat as much as any other animal. There is still the urge to run back to that warm dining room and finish him. I try to push that thought, that instinct away, and concentrate instead on the branches beneath my feet as I traverse the paths of the canopy, coming more and more clear in the faint dawn light.

Suddenly I stop. Another scent has made itself known. Deer. I spot it quickly: a stag, quietly foraging through the undergrowth. His antlers form a spiky crown on his dignified head, and I can see the muscles in his wide shaggy throat as he gazed about him, checking his surroundings, before bending down towards the earth.

He never got a chance to take a bite of the grass.

Pounce. Swipe. Bite.

Beat, beat, sigh, silence.

Eat.

Awareness floods my mind, and I rise from his ravaged neck in horror, an animal driven by hunger, always hunting for the next kill. I had always been blissfully unaware of what my animal side did on my hunts time and time again, but now, aware of my maw smeared in sweet-smelling blood, I have to face what I have become, what I now am. The tearing of meat, the snarling, the sharp claws; there is no escape from it, only acceptance.

My stomach strains from the weight of my meal as I sit back on my haunches. A part of me wants to howl, mark my place in this world and forget again, but the energy escapes me as I think again of the man, in my castle, eating at my table. I envy him and his unknown life, but I would not expose myself to him. I was not meant to mingle with humanity. I would not darken his vision, but let him go home, as I would go home.

Rubbing my jaw and nose in the grass and leaving dark streaks of blood, the deer carcass catches my eye. Even ravaged, he is noble, his eyes not wide with fear, but calm, accepting, seeing farther than I could. I bow my head and touch my horns to his crown of antlers. Then I begin to walk slowly back home.

Even with my engorged stomach slowing my pace, it is not long before I see the familiar gates. Instead of going through, I walk along the path outside the wall towards the gardens. I have not entered them in many moons, finding little joy in seeing the once colorful flowers now only in shades of grey, the many scents combining in the air and making it difficult to smell out my surroundings. But it is away from the main gates, so it is a safe place to stay and wait for the man to leave.

I enter under the thick arching hedge, and the multifold scents assail me. I inhale shallowly and continue through the low bushes lining the curving path. The garden was built in the shape of two crescents with a circle between them, moons flanking suns, and paths weaving through them like rays of light. I follow the path to the tip of one moon, the tiny flowers nearly as white as stars, then down a sun beam lined with flat faced daisies that I'm sure are yellow, but look merely a warm light grey.

At the center of this garden are roses, in hundreds of shades progressing from light to dark as they near the center of the sun. The sheer mass of roses, their different scents mingling into one heady aroma, overpower everything. I lay down in the curve of the moon with my eyes closed, letting the scent of the roses seep into me and making thought impossible. The new sun spilling on my shoulders, the heady fragrance and my heavy gut combine to lull me into a dazed half-sleep. Everything fades away in the darkness of my mind, and I can almost forget – *no more man.*

Man gone.

Alone.

SNAP like ice on a frozen river cracking, like the heart of a tree breaking, and without thought I issue a loud challenging roar that hurts even my ears. I leap to the center of the garden, rose petals flying before my lowered head. I can feel the earth crumbling beneath my claws, my lips curling back over my teeth in a snarl, the rumble like thunder in my chest and my heavy pelt standing at attention along my spine. Whatever had entered the garden would not remain there long.

Cowering on the ground before me with a broken branch of roses is the man. My growing roar is shocked back down my throat, and to my amazement, what came out was not an animal growl, but words. "Why?"

The man cries out as though I'd dealt him a blow. I resist the urge to cry out too, from surprise and amazement. When was the last time I had spoken human words aloud? It must have been years and years of silence, yet the knowledge hadn't left me in all that time. I turn my attention back to the man, who has started to murmur half formed words in breathless terror. I speak once again, "Why? You... here?" The voice is unfamiliar, and yet I can hear in it something of myself around the rolling thunder that accompanies every syllable. To my way of thinking, it is somewhat of a miracle that this mouth is equipped to speak understandable words, though obviously not in a long while as I struggle to get out my thoughts coherently.

During all this time, the man has not moved. I lean forward, listening to his mumbling; I can faintly make out prayers to numerous gods. I'd talked to them all before, I doubted they would answer now. I chuckle, which sounds like another growl from my mouth, and the man's head snaps up, his lips frozen. The look of sheer terror on his face dismisses any humor. I continue to gaze at him silently, and when he coughs up a few words I realize that he believed I was waiting for the answer to my question, which I had quite forgotten.

"On my way home, I...lost, lost in the Woods, and the storm, I...this place, shelter..." he stammers in a voice as brittle as the autumn trees. I nod, and his mouth clamps shut.

"You found my castle," I say, as softly as I could, slowly picking my words. "You needed warmth... shelter. No one comes here, but you... stayed."

"A generosity...that did not go unnoticed by myself...I assure you," he says, his voice stilted as if it pained him to draw breath. I understand his tension too well; one false move towards this man and he will lose his sanity entirely, or flee. And I would let him run, though I desperately wish to converse with him with my newly rediscovered voice. I slowly take a half step back and sit on my haunches, willing my muscles to relax, the claws to retract. The man does not move, but I can smell his terror abating, curiosity and confusion welling up.

I venture to speak again. "It was not... my choice to let you stay." Let my words ring honest, there is no sense in lying to this man. "And dinner was...unexpected."

"I apologize, if I ate food that was intended for you-" he blurts out. When my tail absently thumps against the ground by my feet, he halts in silence.

"It was for... you. My tastes are... different."

He nods, the muscles around his neck relaxing. Though his eyes still scream out, his body seems tired of the continued strain of fear. He is no longer prostrated before me, but more or less upright on his knees. He still has to look up to see my face, but he seems rather glad of the distance. I look down at the ground and see the branch of roses, forgotten between us.

"Why did you take them?" I ask.

A new terror slips behind his eyes. "I had not thought...I should have known, they had to be yours, but I thought you would not mind, what are a few roses in a garden such as this?"

A few of the flowers have just begun to bud, the dark leaves splitting to reveal the silky petals folded beneath. None are fully open yet. They have never opened. The gardens are frozen in time, like the Wood around them. Those flowers that have bloomed would never die; those branches that were bare would never have new buds. I consider them mournfully.

The man must have read my gaze. "I am sorry for the loss of your roses. I will surely compensate you for them, whatever price."

"You cannot place a price on the roses," I softly growl, confused, my words coming clearer. What is a metal coin compared to the growth of a newly budding rose?

But he is persistent, beginning to ramble. "Anything at all, you shall receive it. I wish to have no ill will between us. Let me erase this debt, I've recently come into a tidy sum, and surely we can come to some arrangement, and then I shall vacate your property, just leave and it will be like I had never come here."

But my slowly awakening human mind is somewhere else, puzzling out the roses. Why did the man need roses? There is a pale band of skin on his forefinger, possibly from a wedding ring, but no ring there now. Not for a wife, then. And he clearly does not know much about roses, to break off a newly budding branch, instead of a few larger blooms with stems that he could keep damp on the journey.

"Who are the roses for?" I interrupt his stream of words. He grows still, his hands trembling. I look into his face, but his eyes are cast down at the roses. "My youngest daughter, Rosalind. Rose, for short."

"You have daughters?"

"She just asked for a rose, and in my travels, I could not find any. I was so excited at finding them here, I broke off the whole branch. I'd give her a garden like this, if I could. She likes pretty things, she's such a pretty girl. All my daughters, beautiful as the day is long. They're waiting for me back home, for I've been gone many months. I've worried about them, all alone."

His words are coming faster, his tone nearly hysterical and his breath coming in short bursts. In hopes to calm him, I ask, "Tell me about them, your daughters."

A smile threatens the corner of the man's mouth, and he takes a deep breath before speaking again. "Three I have, no sons, but I do not consider it a loss. My eldest, Giselle, never a more elegant woman on this earth. Hair like the raven's plumage, emerald eyes, and tongue sharp as a dagger. More than one over-confident lad has found himself pierced by her wit and cunning. More experienced in the world than I would like, perhaps, but what manner of father would I be to deprive and restrain her confidence?

"My beauty though, my Rose, she I should like to keep close to me always. The last child of my late wife, and she reminds me of her more and more each day. The same long, golden hair, and her eyes are a blue as brilliant as the sky. Already so beautiful for such a young age, she'll soon surpass her sisters, if she hasn't already. She illuminates the room simply by walking in. Any man would gladly have her for her beauty alone. She stays, though, doting on an old man."

He pauses, smile forgotten on his face. Overwhelmed by his words and the fervor with which he spoke them, a random thought crosses my mind and escapes through my lips. "You have another daughter?"

Something flashes in his eyes, and the wandering gaze left them, replaced by the previously repressed anxiety and fear. "Yes, my second eldest, Evelyn."

Three daughters...he continues to speak, but a selfish, awful, hypnotizing plan has begun to form in my mind. The man has daughters, and is in my debt, our worlds colliding in a garden full of roses - these things cannot be coincidence. But how could it ever possibly work? The only method of persuasion I have anymore is fear, but would that be enough?

I drag my attention back to the man. He has fallen silent, eyes expectant. Then, in answer to my horrendous dilemma, he asks, "What can I give you, in exchange for these roses? I know they are valuable to you, with all the care you've put into this garden. What would you ask of me?"

No matter how civil I could act, I know what he see when he looks at me. He humors me, speaks to me, only because he fears death. The roses are all he desired, and they are all I have to bargain with. He will never agree to what I am about to ask. But I have to try.

"I need no coin or treasure. But I'm lacking in...company. You are the first man that has spoken to me in many years. Take the roses to your daughter. They will bloom...for a time. When they begin to die, I will take my payment... either you, or one of your daughters, must come back."

I keep my gaze steady on him, waiting for him to run, to fight, to attempt to call my bluff. Surely he knows that if I haven't attacked him yet, I will not now. He will run, I will not chase him, and this world will fade behind him, myself included. He and I both know it is too much to ask in exchange for flowers.

But he does none of these things. His mouth is open, the words he wants to say frozen. His eyes shake, his whole body shakes. He seems to fade before my eyes, like death is passing over him.

Even as I cause this pain, I try to lessen it, forcing my mouth to say exactly what I need to say. "No harm will befall your daughter, on my honor. She will be well cared for here, have whatever she requests. And your family will be well compensated. I only seek a reprieve from my loneliness." Will he notice, how I refer to his daughters, and not himself? Will it become transparent that I really wish for one of his daughters to return? But he does not seem the kind of man who would sacrifice his children to save his own life. Yet, I can't press the ultimatum of one of his daughters on him, no matter how much I wish to. I have to give them the choice.

The man seems frozen, unable to comprehend what I said to him. Yet, he must have heard, because slowly, as though it takes all his willpower, he nods. However, the look on his face throws the cruel act I have committed back at me, no matter how much I try to rationalize it. I can't bear to look at the man I have decimated. "Go," I nearly growl. "Make your choice. And don't think to deny me, for I will come and find you!"

He nods once more, but makes no other move. I cannot take it anymore. "Go!" I cry out, a roar issuing from my throat, and the man shoots up, roses clasped in his hand, and flees. It isn't until the sound of his footsteps have faded away that my roar dies, and I fall down to the ground in horror at what I had done. I now cowered as the man had, before the beast that I had let control me. And yet, no matter how horrible I feel, a small part of my mind would keep its humanity, now that it knew there was hope. There was a chance.

FOUR

SECRETS

It was the fearful pitch in Rose's "Father!" that made me run down the stairs to her, Giselle right behind. He stood in the doorway, soaked through from the rain hammering down behind him, a cloth bundle in his arms like a child. I rushed forward, took the bundle from Father's arms. He let it go willingly, placed his empty hands on Rose's shoulders. She led him to his chair by the fire, slowly, and for once I did not doubt Rose's exaggerated care. He did not seem to know there was a floor beneath his feet, every step unsteady. "He'll need dry clothes," Giselle said to no one in particular, then walked into Father's room. I made sure Rose was in control and then stepped into the kitchen to heat some water for tea. I set the bundle on the table. It was surprisingly light for its size, and it had several angles that had poked my arms. I filled the kettle, set it over the hearth, and pulled out mugs, tea leaves, milk, some of our precious honey, all the while keeping an open ear towards the parlor. I heard Rose and Giselle murmuring, the rustle of fabric and thud of boots, the splatter of water drops.

Soon enough the kettle whistled, and I quickly filled the cups and brought the tray out. Father's cloak hung by the door, a pool of water forming beneath it. He was covered in blankets that Giselle tucked around him, his feet nearly in the fire, and still he shivered. I quickly passed Rose his cup, which she pressed to his lips. He managed to swallow, and that seemed to do him good, as his shivers subsided. He looked around at his daughters hovered around him, seeming to just notice us. "My dears," he said, his voice strained, like he had been shouting before he'd come to our door. "My precious girls." And we were all hugging him, and he held us all, and I couldn't remember the last time any of us had embraced each other so naturally.

After we had parted, we pulled the chairs closer together, the warmth of the fire flowing over all of us. We sipped the tea quietly, our glances alighting on each other. I felt like I was seeing my family anew, in the glow of the flames. Giselle looked softer, her mouth not so tight, her sharp eyes more rounded. The lines in Father's face were deeper, shadowed ravines across his forehead and around his mouth, and I could see the years that lay on him. And Rose, Rose was even more beautiful. It didn't matter what light or what situation you saw her in, she always looked lovely. And yet, it was not a beauty befitting her years. She seemed to look too mature, too soon.

But none of these things could mask the tension in all our shoulders, the tight fingers gripping our mugs. We felt the unknown swirling around us. Father's sudden appearance, the mysterious bundle, his inability to stop shivering, even now — something had happened, beyond the storm.

Giselle was the first to ask. "Father, what happened to you? You should have not been back for days."

"And why did you travel on foot, in this weather?" Rose chimed in. "You should have gone with a caravan, gotten a horse at least."

A sudden thought gripped my heart, and I wished my sisters would stop asking him questions, for I now dreaded what the answers would be.

Father placed his mug down, his hand withdrawing beneath the blankets. His face remained stoic, but his eyes betrayed him. "I am so sorry, my dears."

My head fell forward, and remained that way as he told us what I had feared: there was nothing left of the Heron. Cargo long gone, if there ever was any, the ship had been reduced to the bare bones, so he sold it for parts. It was a meager sum, but it alerted some of his creditors that he was back in the city, and he was forced to leave less than a fortnight after he'd arrived. When he told us a new house stood where ours once had, we were not surprised, but that didn't soften the pain.

The weather held for most of the trip, but a day's journey out of Magnasaltus, the storm descended as the sun did, and he was forced to take shelter in the Wood. He thought he was following the straight path, the one he had always told us to take, but somewhere along the way, he'd taken a wrong step, and found himself deeper and deeper in the Wood. The rainwater flooded everything, making it impossible for him to tell that he had crossed the river until he found himself at a gate.

I found myself interrupting, "A gate? No one lives in the Wood."

Father looked at me strangely, and then said, "That is what I thought, Evelyn. I assumed it was old, an abandoned settlement. But that meant shelter, so I entered, and found it was the gate to a castle."

"A castle?" I knew Giselle's ears would perk at that. "But there is no record of a ruling wealthy family near Magnasaltus." I saw her swallow, no doubt holding back a hundred questions, but Father held up a hand, and she fell back in her chair, silent again.

"Nearly the moment I stepped through the gate, the rain abated, and I could see the castle looming before me. I got the sense it was immense in all directions, though I couldn't see very far in the dark, and I was too glad to see something with a roof, so I went under the entryway, and found the door ajar. When I went inside, it was only dimly lit by the windows high above, but then there was a flash of light, and I turned around to see a roaring fire in the fireplace."

I felt everyone in the room stiffen, but no one asked who had started the fire. "There was a long table, and a place set for one, only one chair. The rest of the room was empty, and I stood by the fire, warming myself, pretending this was all normal. But then...then I turned around, and the table was full with dishes, tureens, pitchers, and the air was full of delicious smells. But, I heard no one come in, heard no clinking of silver or dishes being set down. But there must have been someone..." he trailed off, lost in some thought.

Giselle finally ventured to break the silence. "You mean to say someone is living there, in the castle?"

Father nodded. "I waited for him to appear for some time. But he never did, and I had to assume that the food was for me. When I sat down and pulled the first dish toward me, it was still hot. After I finished, I leaned back in the chair a moment, eyes closed; only a moment I was sure. But when I opened my eyes, there was a divan to my right, laden with blankets and a pillow. I was so exhausted, I was sure I'd fallen asleep momentarily at the table, and that someone had brought in the divan then. Clearly, they were not meant to be seen, and I was reminded of our old life, where our food appeared on our plates as if by magic, and when we went up to our rooms to sleep, the sheets were already turned down and the fire banked. An efficiently run house, that one."

I felt a twinge of loss at remembering the comfort of our old life. I still missed having the bed already warm when I crawled into it.

Rose's voice jolted us out of our reverie. "So your host didn't show himself?"

"Not that night. When I awoke the next morning, there was breakfast on the table, still just one place setting. I haven't eaten so well in a long time. After I ate, I tried to explore the castle, see if I could find and thank my host. It was a beautiful place. But most of the doors were locked, and the farther I went into the place, the more I felt that I was intruding.   So   I   left."

There was more, though. That was not the end of this story. "It took you a whole day to get back?" I asked. Rose looked shocked at my impertinence, but Father nodded. "I was still a day out, remember? All that wandering in the Wood didn't get me very far."

"What about what you were carrying?" I asked further. "What is it?"

"Presents can wait!" Rose chastised me.

But Father placed a hand on her shoulder. "It's alright, Rose. Go bring it in here."

When Rose had placed it in Father's lap, his hands hovered over the bindings for a moment. "It might not have lasted the trip," he warned us. "I wasn't thinking about it…it probably didn't survive." But he untied the cords, and pulled away the cloth.

"Oh, Father," Rose whispered, her hands involuntarily reaching to touch. In Father's lap lay a branch of roses, beautiful blooming roses, in so many colors – soft pink, icy white, classic red, yellow with orange blushes. I did not know that so many different types of roses could grow on one branch, until I realized that it was not one branch, but a kind of woven wreath, each different color of rose on its own separate stem.

"Oh, Father," Rose hushed again, "where did you get them? They are beautiful."

"And so many kinds," Giselle said, her hands also gravitating towards the blossoms.

"A gift from my host," said Father, but I was sure I could detect a faint note of disappointment in his voice, as though he'd wished the roses hadn't survived. But I couldn't imagine why, they were indeed beautiful. Each one seemed frozen at the perfect moment in their blooming. The pink ones were fully opened, nearly flat in a profusion of cloudy petals. The red ones were traditionally scrolled, the white ones tight, barely parting at the top.

Rose had already separated a strand of roses, mainly pink, with yellow seeping in at the edges of the petals, and deepening to a rich orange at the base. Giselle was detaching the strand of pure white blooms, her delicate fingers careful around the thorns. I went into the kitchen, filled the largest pitcher we had with water, and returned to the parlor. I placed the rest of the roses in the jar, and Rose came over to help me arrange them so each stem had a chance at the water beneath it. We exchanged a small hidden smile, unable to remain at odds with such beautiful flowers before us.

"I wonder how they have bloomed so early in the year," I wondered aloud.

"I was just thinking that myself," said Rose. "It is difficult enough to get roses to bloom in high summer, so to part from such rare blooms is indeed a great gift."

"A very generous gift, to be sure," Giselle said behind us. "Too bad he couldn't have thrown in a few silver chains to tie them together." But her voice had none of its usual bite, and I turned to see her still gazing at the roses in her hands.

Father stood suddenly, and we all looked up at him expectantly. But he only announced he was going to bed, and after assuring Rose that he was well enough on his own, he went to his room and shut the door. We continued sitting there for a while, unwilling to break the impromptu peace between us that the roses had brought. Giselle was the first to leave, stifling a yawn as she went to our room. I wished to say something to Rose, to talk about something harmless and preserve whatever that small smile had meant, but I stayed silent while Rose went and checked in Father's room to make sure he'd gotten to bed, then went to her own room.

I knew that I should get to bed as well, that my day started early. But there was something soothing about the fire, the light rain falling on the roof, the serene roses. I jolted myself out of my reverie, thinking about having to get more water from the well tomorrow, most likely in the rain. As I placed the pitcher on the mantle, something dark fell from it onto the floor, and I stooped down to grab it, perhaps a leaf, or fallen petal.

It was neither of those things, but a rose, unlike any other rose in the bundle Father had brought. Indeed, it was unlike any rose I had seen in my whole life. I crouched nearer the fire, to see it better. It perfectly fit the contour of my cupped hand, the petals so plush they felt like velvet. And it was the exact shade of the midnight sky, a black so rich it looked blue. I held it to my face and inhaled.

It smelled like a rose, but it also smelled like rushing water, like the silver of stars. For a moment I was no longer kneeling on the floor of the parlor, but standing on the edge of a river. I could feel the kiss of water on my cheeks as mist swirled around me, and above the stars blazed bright as fire.

And just as suddenly, I was back in the parlor, the rose laying quietly in my hand, as roses do. I set it on the arm of my chair softly, and busied myself with banking the fire. In the dim light, I took the rose up to my room, where I silently changed into my sleeping dress. Giselle was asleep, the white roses woven around her headboard. Unwilling to let my rose dry out like hers, I set it in my water basin. The stem rested on the bottom of the bowl and curved up the side to let the head peek over the edge. I lay down in bed, for once unheeding of the cold sheets against my body, and lay on my side to look at the rose. It seemed to grow, a darkness that expanded until it covered my vision and I slept.

When I came downstairs early next morning, I found someone already in the kitchen. Father sat at the table, hands folded, head bowed. I stopped in the doorway, not wanting to interrupt him. But he looked up and waved me in. "It's very early for you to be up, Father. Would you like me to get you some breakfast?"

"Just some bread and jam, if we can spare."

"Of course," I said, and turned to the cabinets, busying myself with the preparation. The unfamiliarity of the situation made me nervous. I could not recall the last time I had been alone with my father.

As I placed the plates on the table, he reached over and put a hand on my outstretched wrist. "Evelyn, it may be selfish of me, the demand I am about to make of you. But you are a good girl, a sensible girl, and I need another mind to help me with an important decision."

"Of course, Father," I said, astonished. Was he really taking me into his confidence? "Anything I can do for you."

"Thank you daughter," he said relieved, as though a weight had been lifted off him, and released my hand. I turned back to the counter, taking a knife to cut the bread. Belied by my newfound assurance, I asked, "Does this have to do with your journey home, Father?"

"Indeed, it does. You were right to be suspicious of me last night. Perhaps it was not appropriate for you to question me like that..." and I froze, knife hovering above the crust. But he continued, "...but you deserve to be told the truth, since you did ask." I sliced the bread in thick hunks and brought it to the table with the jams, sitting down cattycorner from him. The unspoken truth lay heavy between us, and I was glad to have something to do while I waited for him to voice it. I spread a little strawberry jam on a piece, and took a small bite, chewing slowly.

"After I left the castle, I did a little more searching. The day had turned beautiful, and there was no sense that I was intruding, as there was inside. I found a park of sorts, walked the paths for some time. I confess I forgot that I was looking for anyone, and just began to enjoy my surroundings. It is was the kind of thing your mother and I would have done when we were courting." I swallowed my bread abruptly. Father rarely talked about Mother, and with great pain when he did so. He spoke now fondly, a happy remembrance.

"I did not know Mother enjoyed gardens," I said carefully, not wishing to invoke one of his moody silences. But he merely shook his head, smiling. "She loved flowers, partly because she knew I'd compare them to her beauty, and find them wanting. But she also loved them for their scents, their perfumes."

"Like lavender."

"Yes, that was one of her favorites. She liked to gather it herself, dry and crush it and sew little packets of it to place in her dresses." I had not known that, although it should have been obvious to me, but in my young years, I had assumed she naturally smelled like that.

"I didn't find any lavender in the garden. Throughout the air, there was a heady aroma that overpowered all other smells. As I approached what I assumed was the center of the park, the scent grew stronger, till I turned a corner, and found the source, a garden filled with roses. Every color of rose, in every scent. It was staggering. I believe I was unable to move for quite some time. And then, I remembered your sister, and her request for a rose."

I winced at the reminder of Rose's request, and the terrible silence that had followed till Father came home. I took another bite of bread as Father continued with his tale. "I was returning with nothing, just as I had left with nothing. I thought to at least fulfill Rose's desire. I thought you would all enjoy them, not as much as the jewels I sought to bring you, of course, but they were something. So I broke off the branch.

"The sound…the sound of the branch breaking echoes in my mind even now. It went beyond sound. It was like something inside me was breaking. I knew that I had committed a terrible act, had done something irrevocable before he even spoke."

"He?" I whispered, leaning towards Father.

"Can I even refer to him that way?" he mused, a flash of terror passing across his face. "He...it was... a shadow with sharp claws, sharper teeth...monstrous."

I shivered. "How did you escape alive, unharmed?" I asked, and then something else pushed itself to the forefront of my mind. "It spoke?"

"In words that you and I could understand."

"What did it say?"

"It asked why I had come to his castle, and I told him of the storm, and thanked him profusely for his hospitality. And then he asked why I had picked the roses, and I could not help myself, I had to tell him the truth. I told him about Rose, about all of you..." His voice hitched on what could have been mistaken for a sob, except my Father did not cry. Not even at Mother's funeral had he cried.

"And then he told me what price I was to pay for the roses. Either I, or one of my daughters, was to return to him, and remain there."

I felt like I had fallen on the stairs, the breath knocked out of me for many moments. "For how long?" I gasped out. "To what end?"

"He said he was...lonely. But what words of a creature such as he are to be trusted? He said that no harm would befall my daughters, but for all I know, he will keep us all in that castle for his personal entertainment, and should one of us fail...!"

My mind began to process more. "How long do we have?"

"As long as the roses bloom, he said. Also to get my affairs in order, most likely. I am glad of the time, even if it is just a longer pause before the swing of the executioner's blade. That is why I wish your help, Evelyn."

"How so?" I was now thoroughly confused.

"I need someone with your careful planning and thought to help me decide what to do, about this demand."

I sat in silence for a moment, unsure where to go. As much as the situation terrified me, my mind was strangely calm and clear. I decided to think of the problem as objectively as possible, make it as mundane as a decision on whether to buy a little syrup in town, or tap a maple tree for sap myself. Different choices, different advantages.

"Well, let's look at the possibilities. We don't know that he knows for certain where we live. We could ignore his demand and his deadline."

"And look over our shoulders for the rest of our lives, live in fear of the day when he does arrive at our door? That is no way to live, especially not for you girls."

"Could we...deal with him? Ourselves, or get someone to..." But I silenced my own thought. What man would enter the Wood to hunt a monster? The Wood already had a reputation for being unkind towards the intrusion of man. Add an unknown demon that spoke like a man, and no one would take even the straight path in the Wood again.

Father was shaking his head too. "I would not put that task on any man."

"But then, it seems we have no choice but to send someone to him."

"As I feared," he said solemnly, "and of course it will be me."

"But Father!"

"Do you think I would send one of my daughters to that thing?"

"He said we would not be harmed!"

"He is not human, no matter what words he says, so how can his words be trusted?"

I knew that this was not up for discussion anymore, but I couldn't let him do this. "What of us, what will we do after you are gone? Who will take care of the family?"

He shook his head. "He said that we would be compensated for our loss. But you children have been caring for yourselves for many years now. I know I have been acting the invalid and been a burden for some time, but you have pushed on in spite of that, and I know if I left, in any circumstance, I know you would manage just as you have for years. I admire your loyalty, Evelyn," he said, and he reached across the table to hold my hands, "but right now I ask of you your logic, your reason. I need you to help me craft a story to explain my disappearance to your sisters. I feel guilty as it is for pulling you into this, but I need someone to convince the others not to come searching for me, to know the truth and eventually reveal it when enough time has passed. Please, Evelyn."

My proud father begging for my help in orchestrating this sacrifice overwhelmed me for a moment, pulling a tear from me, but I took a steadying breath and gripped his hands back. "Of course, Father."

We kept the story simple. Father would receive a new message saying another ship had come in, at a more distant city across the waters. He would leave, and somewhere along the journey between the cities, he would be lost at sea. He'd leave behind a sealed letter to be sent back home to us after a few weeks had passed, notifying us of his passing, and our father would be dead to the world and all those in it, but me. And my sisters, if I ever told them what truly happened.

The truth of our situation gripped my mind continually. I couldn't share my feelings with Father. Beyond our planning for his eventual disappearance, nothing had changed in our relationship. The distance between us made me feel alone in the deception of my sisters. It was all I could do at meals not to stand up and scream, to share my burden in hopes that someone would step forward with another plan. But I had only myself to turn to.

When I wasn't working in the house, I stayed out of doors, avoiding the eyes of my family. Most often, I walked the birch path of the Wood, which even now held no terror for me. It was calming, repetitive; to pretend that there was nothing I had to return to. It was one day, the pale sun weakly illuminating the birch, that the thought appeared in my head. I instantly willed it away, having conjured up outrageous plots before. But it had already imprinted on me, left a glimmer of hope, or fear. What if I went in Father's place?

"Completely insane," I muttered, pausing to smooth my skirts, an action foolish in our new life of common cloth, but still familiar. "Utterly ridiculous." But it didn't feel ridiculous. It felt...right. This beast had asked for someone to return. Why could it not be me? The fact that Father had come back, physically unscathed, meant that this thing had some sense of decency. It also meant that Father was not whom the beast wanted, otherwise he could have kept Father his captive. Giselle would not even consider the risk, and Father would never let his Rose go. But what of me? I was little more than a servant in that house as it was, any able maid could fulfill my duties. And no matter what Father said about our capabilities, three young women without the presence of a man would not be proper, not to mention dangerous. It made more than enough sense that I should be the one who went to the beast.

Father's description of the creature did make me shiver, though maybe that was the autumn winds, or the darkness lurking under the trees behind the birch, thick and wild as pythons. I remembered the traveling menagerie, the dragons and unicorns, the gryphon, gold as the sun with a wingspan as long as a man's reach. All those creatures had been in bright, glittering colors, intended to dazzle and bewilder. But what of a monster that couldn't be seen until it was already on you?

And yet, I was curious. How did its limbs move when it ran? How did it speak, and what did its voice sound like? I had once heard a small dragon that had been trained to speak. It spoke in monotones, each syllable like the hiss of lava hitting cold water. The dragon was only repeating like a parrot, unaware of what the words meant, but this thing did not sound like that. Could he have been educated?

And I began to laugh. I laughed at the branches overhead, at the sun, at myself. What did it matter? A beast is a beast. And it was very unlikely I would ever meet it myself, to find the answers to my questions. Completely unlikely, since the idea of me going in Father's place was absurd. I knew I shouldn't entertain these thoughts, that I should follow Father's plan.

But I do not always do as he says.

Every moment brings a new level of despair for the lives I am ruining, followed by the sharp pains of hope. The fact that I dare to hope, frightens me. But hope drives me through the castle, looking at ceilings for leaks, testing staircases that I would usually leap over, standing in the center of rooms, feeling for drafts. Too many thoughts confuse my mind, long accustomed to singular, overriding instinct, but I manage to stumble through and focus on practical matters – is there enough firewood for the winter, can the bed sheets be salvaged, does the kitchen have any cooking pots? There are times I want to drop down where I stand, but sudden thoughts send me back down the halls, beating the draperies with my tail to release decades of dust. After the stilted dialogue with her father, I practice speaking with my new voice, releasing one-sided conversations into the silence while I work.

As the sun rises ever higher in the sky, though, I find that more and more problems are solved, without my doing. Doors that have been closed since I arrived now stand ajar, the rooms inside light and airy from open windows. Sheets that I hang out windows and balconies are refitted around beds. On the rare occasions I stop at the dining room to eat, there are two places set at the table. By the time the candles begin to light themselves in their sconces, I knew I had severely underestimated the abilities of the spirits that dwelled here, though I do not know how they ascertained that someone was coming. Perhaps they understood my human words, as well as animal instincts. They even manage to conjure up coins and gold, enough for a kingdom, to compensate the family for the loss of their daughter and sister. With their help, the day comes where the sun has finally crests over the trees, and I know with certainty that time is up.

Rose had become suspicious. Despite Father's recovery and seeming good spirits, she doted on him more than usual, slipping reassurances in with his tea. When she came in on Father and I sitting in the kitchen, where we had been discussing further nuances of his plan, she kept her eyes on me, even as she further plied Father about his health. She refused to outright demand to know what was going on, but I saw the uncertainty beneath her face. The distance from Father and the hostility from Rose make it impossible for me to let go of my own plan, my insane, impossible plan to leave and be my family's savior. As the weeks progressed though, my plan became less about saving the others, and more about saving myself. There were so many things wrong with my plan, not the least of which was quite possibly my death, that I should have forgotten it long ago. But it haunted my dreams. He haunted my dreams, the beast, darker and larger than the night, his glowing eyes smoldering before me. He never chased or attacked me; he just loomed above, blending with the sky. One night, he opened his mouth, and a black-blue rose was nestled between his teeth. Before I could pluck it from his jaws, I woke up, my hand suspended above the rose beside my bed. I lay back in bed, arms clasped beneath the sheets, wondering why I'm not as afraid as I should be.

All too soon, the day arrived where Father entered the house with a letter in his hand. I listened intently with the others as he said another of his ships had arrived in port. Again, I helped with the preparations, putting together some food for his travels, laundering clothes so he'd have something nice to wear. It was late afternoon when Rose entered the kitchen, where I was salting some beef I bought from the butchers yesterday. She stood in the corner as I continued to rub the salt into the meat and tried to ignore her.

"There is no ship, is there?"

I continued to rub. "What do you mean?"

"I mean that there is no ship of Father's waiting at port. The last time he went, there was nothing left, and he had to flee before he was seized and thrown in debtor's prison. There wouldn't be enough treasure on that ship to appease his creditors."

"Maybe there is."

"Honestly Evelyn, who do you think you're fooling here? If there were such a ship, Father still wouldn't risk it, he'd send someone else to go inspect it. To go again, just on the heels of his last trip, where he almost died in the Wood-"

"But he didn't die. In fact, it seems he was well cared for."

"So he says! It is unlike me to be suspicious of Father, but there is something he's not telling us, something he's hiding."

I pounded a corner of the beef, tenderizing it. "Why would Father hide something from us? He's in the dark as much as we are about that castle. Stop worrying."

"I should have expected this attitude from you. It's easy to see how distant you are with Father, how you can't even meet his eye at times. But I would have thought you cared enough about him to see something is troubling him."

I picked up the slab of meat and flipped it over more forcefully than necessary, feeling some of the blood spray onto my arms and chin. "Rose, if you're so sure that something is wrong, then go ask Father. Don't come attacking me. What is going on with him is not up to me, so either make him tell you, or leave it alone."

"It's not right for me to demand that of Father."

"Then leave it alone," I said, slamming my hands on the table.

She hesitated, no doubt readying herself for another retort about me being a poor excuse for a daughter, when Giselle walked in, an empty cup in her hands. After a moment, Rose spun on her heel and left the kitchen. I thought for a moment about following her, but decided that she wouldn't listen to me anyways.

"Always so dramatic, isn't she?" Giselle said haughtily, waltzing over to the fireplace and peering inside the kettle to see if the water was boiling. I merely nod, wiping the blood off my hands to pour tea. Dramatic, yes, but determined. I had no doubt Father would give in to her, if she asked the right questions. Soon only Giselle would be in the dark, and even that wouldn't last for long. She was giving me looks similar to the ones Rose had been giving me. I wanted to hold her hand, tell her everything, have her talk me out of the actions I was about to attempt and hug her tightly till I forgot the last year. I did nothing but hold my mug. Despite the calming tea, my pulse raced, and when Giselle finally left and headed to bed, I nearly jumped out of my chair and ran to the back door, where the bag I had supposedly been packing for Father lay. I pulled out the shirts and pants, and placed the fresh bread and fruits inside. My thoughts were a blur, running before me so fast I had no hope of catching them and could only chase after them. I shouldered the bag and brought it to the front door, grabbed my cloak, then paused. Across the room I could see light from under Father's door, and shadows as feet passed in front of it. At the top of the stairs, Rose's room was empty and dark. I couldn't hear any voices, but I knew what they were talking about. It was a matter of time now before Rose got the answers she wanted. I sat down by the fireplace, holding my cloak and a threaded needle as if I were just catching up on some sewing repairs. Let Rose come out, see me there, argue with me if she must, and then go to bed. Then, I would leave. Father and Rose would be happy and safe, and Giselle would never know how close we had been to another disaster.

Sitting still worried me though, gave my thoughts a chance to slow down and make me reconsider. I concentrated on the banking fire, the little spurts of flame that cracked the logs and sent showers of sparks into the chimney. I imagined the darkness of the Wood, the impenetrable dark, punctuated only by two pinpricks of smoldering light. Each second was a second closer to the end, and beginning, of my life.

Years of waking up at dawn prompted my eyes to open as the first flicker of sunlight drifted into the house. I looked down at my hands, still grasping the cloak and needle, and my plan returned, forcing me out of the chair I'd slept in. As I drew the cloak over my shoulders, the image of a blue rose surfaced in my mind. I would bring it with me, a sign of goodwill. I silently crept up the stairs and eased into my room. The rose still floated in the basin, but when I touched it, the petals broke off and fluttered to the floor. I turned to see Giselle's sleeping form covered in fallen white petals, the garland above her bed no more than a thorny bower. She sighed in her sleep, and I quickly left the room, wondering if Rose's flowers had died also. This thought prompted me to open her door, which showed her room bright in the sunlight and empty. The bed was made, her shoes were missing, and rose petals rocked softly on the open windowsill.

I ran down the stairs, not caring about the noise now. The bag I had packed was gone. I burst into Father's room, and shook him by the shoulders till he looked up, bleary eyed at me. "Where is Rose?" I asked him. He didn't give an answer, or seem to understand the question. "Rose, your daughter, where is she?"

"What do you mean?"

"She's gone, Father. She's not here, where is she?"

Recognition dawned on his face, followed by horror. "I told her...I told her what had happened, where I was going..." His hands gripped mine. "She promised me she wouldn't go, she promised..."

I tore myself away, ran out the front door where the Wood, shrouded in mist, stood silently, confirming what I already knew. Rose had gone to the beast.

FIVE

ENCOUNTERS

After weeks of frenetic energy, I am incapable of moving from the balcony above the entrance hall. I can smell fires banking in every room, the absence of dust and dirt. If I were to lean over the balcony, I would see myself reflected in every gleaming tile of the floor. In the same way that I observed her father, I would watch her arrive in hiding. I still did not know how to approach her. Outside in the daylight, she would be spared nothing. Inside, I'd be cloaked in shadows and nightmares. I try to push the worries out of my mind and sit there, quiet, waiting as the sun crests over the trees, and hangs, weightless, for hours. I refuse to lean towards either despair or anxiety. I am sure she spent as long as she could with her family, waiting till the last possible moment to leave them. I am as motionless as if I were waiting for prey to cross my path, startling to consider, but in a way it was true that I was hunting this girl, that I had been hunting her for so long, waiting for her to come to me. In horror I feel my animal nature approve the idea, bones shifting and settling, claws hovering at the edge of my paws. And then, a scream, from far away but at piercing as a needle to my brain and I leap out the open window, eyes straight ahead, running.

Why did I feel betrayed? My family had been saved by my sister's selfless act, and yet I felt just as I had years ago in the center of the ballroom · eclipsed. Could I really be jealous of Rose's generosity, even now? Did I envy her this path? Yes, I did, because I had been serious about going. Even in the light of day I did not think those actions to be foolish. My departure was not a cry for attention, a desire for my father's love. Even the knowledge that it would save my family had been an afterthought. Mingled with the envy was regret, a lamentation that it was not I who was now walking through the Wood towards an uncertain future.

Minutes crawl. At every turn, I was seized by a wild impulse to run after Rose, and I force my shaking limbs to walk back to the task at hand, bread to bake, floors to sweep, to a father stricken with grief and a sister who remains unaware, to certain safety and a predictable future. Giselle stayed close throughout the day, but I barely noticed her talk of Rose's elopement with the rich man who owned the castle Father had stayed at, her own conclusion when confronted with Rose's disappearance. Enough of the facts are similar that I did not correct her, even if I had the presence of mind to do so. And Father was just as distant as I.

I tried to let the housework consume me, but it wasn't even noon when I drifted upstairs to my room, where I gathered up the fallen blue rose petals off the floor. I held them in my cupped hands, having first intended to throw them away, but now unwilling to do so. I placed them on my bed, and reached into the nightstand to find the remnants of my midnight blue dress. They were just scraps that had been left on the sewing room floor during altering, but even in the faintest light the cloth shimmered like the night sky. The petals were still fresh when I began to sew them into the cloth, wrapping them up so each petal was contained in its own little sachet. The delicate work kept my mind occupied, my eyes restricted to the stitching and not to the Wood looming outside my window. With each petal sewn up, I brought them together into a facsimile of the rose that had died, with the original inside it. By the time I knotted the final thread, the moon had begun its ascent into the sky. Nestled in my hand, it looked and felt much like the living one. Even I was impressed with the final result, and I held it up to my face, wondering if the scent had permeated the fabric.

And then I was walking, drawn down the stairs and out the door by the silver scent of roses and stars, passing through the dim glow of firelight into the rolling darkness. Something led me past the birches, down, deep into the Wood. I let myself get drawn into this silver scent, as tangible as a thread around my wrist, winding towards some unknown end. The loss of control had robbed me of any fear I may have had, and gave me a sense of adventure, of anticipation for what waited for me, and a sad, sweet remembrance of the last time I had come this far. When the sound of rushing water reached me through the trees, I knew I had been expecting it. The late summer storms had swollen the river, swirling by in a profusion of silver. I was aware enough to know that the water would be cold and deep, but it was just another journey, something to discover. There was a jagged line of rocks cresting the water, a makeshift path across the river. The cloth rose shone like a fallen star through my fingers as I looked down at my mercifully booted feet, and I tucked the rose into my bodice. It felt warm against my skin, and I took heart at the rush of excitement as I stepped onto the first rock. It was easy going, the water seeming as innocuous as silk ribbons and starlight. The spray on my cheeks was refreshing, and the other side was close. And then, in one misstep, the friendly river roared with hunger and leapt up to drag me under.

I broke the surface screaming, the water stinging my exposed skin as I flail. It was sheer luck that I grabbed hold of an exposed rock, refusing to release it as the water pummeled me and dragged at my hair and dress. I wrenched my other arm out of the water, grabbed the rock, and hauled myself onto it, legs still treading. The water rushing by blinded me, and my numbed fingers reached out for the next rock. Inch by inch, I battled against the river, until I felt the riverbed rise up beneath me, and the water ebb to a crawl. I frantically climbed out of the water onto the grass, breathing too fast and still unable to catch my breath. Violent shivers rippled over me. There was no escape from the cold piercing my body, and when I desperately opened my eyes, there was utter darkness above me, except for two pinpricks of silver light, and then those faded too.

I'm above her before I can stop myself, just as I had been unable to keep away when I heard the scream through the trees. Her eyes are closed, her hair twisted across her face. I inhale, but her scent is lost in the water that soaks her whole body. Her legs are still in the river, and shudders interrupt her ragged breathing. I take her upper arm carefully in my mouth, and slowly pull her out of the river, careful not to touch the water. Even still, my paw nearest the bank goes numb, and the high-pitched buzzing in my head only fades as I pull her away, to the cover of the trees. I settle her in a cluster of tree roots, her head resting to the side on a bed of moss. Her long hair flutters over her mouth, and I push it back with my nose, revealing a pert nose, a full and slightly crooked mouth, a face dusted with water droplets and as stunning as a star. Her eyes flutter open, and look up at me, unfocused, before they closed with a sigh as she sinks into unconsciousness. The eyes give her away, unchanged after all these years - the girl who danced by the river. Why is she here again, after all this time, on today of all days? It must be a coincidence.

She shifts, and something dark falls from her. I nudge it with one paw, and it turns over, revealing itself in the shape of a rose. Even wet, it looks real, like one of my roses, and instinctively I smell it.

Its scent sends me reeling back. It is one of my roses, or at least it smells like it. Which means...this is her, the traveler's daughter. My prisoner. My salvation. This is no coincidence. This is fate.

I should go. She is out of immediate danger, and she could wake up at any moment, free to continue on her way to me. But she is still soaked, shaking, and daylight is far off here. I can't drag her by the arm all the way through the Wood. There's nothing for it. I lay down beside her, my back to her, and rest my head on my paws. I feel the dampness of her soaking into my fur, but it takes a lot to make me cold, and slowly, she begins to dry and warm. The shudders slow, replaced with soft breaths. Then she moves, more than the gentle movement of sleep, and I bolt up the tree. I peer around the trunk to see her twitching, hands grasping at her legs. One object falls, then another, and she is still again. Only when her breathing deepens do I dare move closer on the branch. Her bare feet glow in the moonlight, her boots discarded on the ground. I am gripped with silent laughter at the utter humanity of this girl, the unconscious mind discarding shoes in sleep. I jump back to the ground, free to go back to a castle that will soon no longer be mine alone, and a garden that is both soothing and troubling. I'm not ready to return to that life, not yet. While the moon stills shines, we still exist in the twilight between a past life of misery and loathing, and an uncertain, yet hopeful, future.

I lay back down at her side, closer than necessary. I drape my tail over her feet, and I feel her curl up against me. Our breathing intertwines in the dark, and I can now taste her scent in the air. On the surface, it is common, comforting, the nearly forgotten scent of baked bread, the salt of a living thing, all too human. But lingering beneath it all is the scent of deep hidden places and the glint of the moon. How long has it been since a living creature touched me, turned to me instead of away? It cannot last, but for the next few hours, these moments are mine.

Daylight woke me, but my eyes were too weak to discern anything other than light, bold white and yellow green. I closed my eyes, and listened to the rush of water nearby. It must be raining outside, but then why was it so bright? I brought a hand up to my head and felt my hair going every direction. I must have tossed and turned all night, and my tired limbs agreed with me. It was long past time for me to be up, but I couldn't bring myself to care. I reached back down for my blanket, remembering a soft shadow of warmth in the night, but instead felt roughness and stalks. I looked down to see dirt, bark, and grass. I was up in an instant, every muscle protesting, but my mind a frantic blur.

I was outside. The sun was shining down through the leaves of the trees above me and glinting off the river flowing past. The night before returned to me, the trance-like journey through the Wood, traversing the river, and falling in. I only remembered making it to the shore, not several feet away at the base of some ancient tree where I had woken up. I run my hands over my body, searching for something wrong. But besides the stiffness of my dress and the tangles in my hair, everything seemed fine. I looked down at my feet and smile. I did remember taking off my shoes in the middle of the night. A small breeze stirred the grass, and something on my feet moved. I leaned in to see hairs, fine dark hairs. Instead of glinting in the sunlight, though, they remained dark. I touched one, and then brushed them off my feet into the grass as I reached for my boots. I was lucky that I wasn't hurt, by the fall or swim to shore. It was more fortunate that I didn't take ill in the night. So close to winter, a night spent outside, and soaked at that, could have had more disastrous results than tangled hair and sore muscles. It should have ended worse. Why didn't it?

Shoes back on, I stood unsteadily, hand on the tree for support. I must have exaggerated the temperature of the water, more shocking than chilling. And with the sun shining, it was hard to imagine that the night had been that cold. It was luck, plain and simple. I eyed the river nervously, but it flowed low and gentle around the rocks, and my excessive care got me back across with no incident. As my feet hit the bank, all the cares and worries descended on me again, and I fled back home.

I leave at first light. The sun illuminates what I could pretend to ignore in darkness, that it was madness to remain near her, that she would find me terrifying no matter what had transpired in the night. Even as she was softly lit in the morning dawn, I remained a darkness that couldn't be leavened.

I reenter the castle like a thief, slink quietly up to my room. No matter the ever-increasing cleanliness of the castle, my room remains the same, dark, broken. It's better that way. At the balcony, surrounded by towers, the glint of windows catching the sun, it's easier to pretend nothing has changed. But my gaze involuntarily flicks to the silver gleam of the river in the distance. Is that particularly tall tree the one I left her under? Does she still sleep? Should I go back? Will she still come?

Within this spiral of doubt, I stare at the midnight blue rose at my feet, the one I took from her while she slept by the river. She had picked this flower, chosen it from all the colors and sewn a flower around it, mingling their scents, somehow weaving us both together. Why would she have done that, and risked the river, if she was not coming? She would be here soon, and I would give this flower back to her, the first of many attempts to redeem myself. I lie beside it, and notice a loose thread at its base. With greater dexterity and patience than I thought possible of me, I push the rose up the side of my face, onto the tip of one of my horns, and slide the thread around it to sit on my head.

Father didn't remark on my absence the next morning, or coming into the kitchen wearing the same clothes I wore yesterday. But Giselle did.

"Where did you go last night?" she bluntly asked as I emerged from the washroom.

"What are you talking about, I was here," I said off-handedly so she didn't question me more. She followed me into our bedroom, where I pulled a new dress out of the wardrobe.

"No you weren't, you weren't in bed this morning." I turned to see her sitting on her bed, arms crossed.

"I had work to do. And you don't even wake up till the sun is high."

"I woke up when you opened the door downstairs last night. I saw you walk across the lawn and into the Wood." She held my gaze as she stood and walked over to me. "And, I definitely saw what your hair looked like before you cleaned yourself up," she added, taking the dress out of my hands.

"What business is it of yours what I do?" I snapped.

"Because I'm your sister."

"You're Rose's sister too, and I don't see you running after her."

"Why would I?" she said, bewildered by my accusatory tone. I sighed and tried to get past her, but she held my shoulders. "Evelyn, what's wrong?"

I considered another stinging remark, but Giselle's innocent face instead moved me to sadness, and a tear escaped me. She sat me down on my bed, knelt before me.

"Yes, Rose is my sister, but we were never as close as you and I are."

"Were."

She pinched my cheek, trying to smile. "Rose made her choice. She left, and I know there is more to it than you are willing to share with me. But you've been listless since she left, since before she left. Ever since Father came home, you've been more distant. Even with Rose gone, you're still angry with her, I can tell. Are you jealous?"

"What?"

"I know I am." She settled next to me on the bed. "What a brilliant plan. Maybe a tad bold, but how could any man resist her?" She caught my blank stare. "It's okay to envy her. She's probably sleeping in till noon on a downy bed, eating quail and salmon, and the dresses, oh!" She fell back on the bed in a swoon. "I can only imagine. I'm sure the mysterious prince is sparing no expense on her. She's probably forgotten all about us, though I would have thought she'd send word to Father, at least. Maybe she's waiting for the wedding before she invites us over."

I fell to the bed beside her in laughter, comparing the idea in Giselle's head to the tale I had heard from Father. Giselle joined in, but then my laughter turned to tears, and Giselle suffered me to cry on her shoulder while I regained composure. When I was calm, she kissed me on the forehead and went back downstairs, leaving me to get dressed, and think about Giselle's jealousy. True, she was jealous of something that I knew did not exist, but she was right. I was jealous of Rose, of her ability since childhood to get what she wanted without effort or consequence, of the way she took from me what I most desired, with no apparent realization of the pain she inflicted on me.

I emerge from my chambers. I wanted to give her the daylight, time to explore, to be enchanted by the beauty of the place. Now, the hallways are bathed in golden candlelight and soft shadows, and I see, far below, the garden illuminated with soft dawn light and hanging lanterns. It is magical even to my eyes; I can only hope that she had seen it the same. I shake my head to twist the rose to hang between my horns and descend the grand staircase, trying to remember grace and decorum, before I smell the fire already banking in the dining room. Both relieved and upset, I still hope she ate well, that she enjoyed what was presented to her. With the large front doors closed, I'll leave through the side door in the dining room. It is only as I'm nudging the door open that I hear the creak of a chair, and realize too late that there is still someone in the dining room. The door swings open into the mercifully dim room. Even before I locate her, I feel her pulse quickening, her blood racing through her body. I stand quietly by the edge of the fireplace, hidden by the flames and the shadows they cast. Into the silence I speak the words I have been practicing since I sent her father away. "Good evening."

After a few moments, she replies, "Good evening, sir."

If my voice is like thunder, her voice is like summer rain – soft, nearly disappearing before it reaches me. "Sir," I snort, unable to stop myself. "You should not call me sir. Call me...Beast." How utterly appropriate. I shift, and I see her shift too, following my movements, hoping and fearing a glimpse of me. Her hair catches the firelight, brighter than I had seen this morning.

"Did you enjoy dinner?" I ask.

"Oh, yes, yes I did, thank you...Beast." Her words are more breath than sound.

"Good. Have you found your rooms to your taste?"

"They are very lovely, thank you." She does not say where they are, and I do not press it. She deserves every secret she chooses to keep, especially the location of where she sleeps. But I wonder if they overlook the rose garden. Would she wish for a reminder of the life she once had, or does she think that looking at the cause of her captivity is the only reward she'll receive?

A sharp gasp alerts me that I leaned forward in thought, my monstrous bulk further illuminated. I straighten up, but know that the inevitable has come. "Why don't we get a better look at each other?" I say, quietly but insistently. In response, her slender shadow slowly stands up from her chair. We are both terrified, and strangely this gives me courage. I step into the wide swath of firelight as she does and look down into her eyes.

No.

This close to her, I do not allow myself a sigh, a growl, any sound or movement to scare. But, no, how can this be? This is not the girl from the river. This is wrong. My throat threatens to explode in rage, and it takes every muscle to force the roar back into my gullet. I've been tricked. What fate would cast a woman in my path, a girl from my past to save, to forge a connection, to hope, only to send another in her place? More than ever before, I feel the weight of my curse binding, constricting, entrapping. What a fool I have been.

I force myself to breathe, to process, to accept and move forward, instead of regressing into the animal that is waiting coiled behind my ribs, ready to spring. Too much time has passed since I last spoke, but the girl still stands before me, frozen like a rabbit in an open field. As I concentrate on her, willing calm into my veins, I see a kind of curtain lift off her, a haze I recognize as spirits that had rushed around her protectively while I internally raged. I cannot tell if she saw them. She is also trying to breathe normally, but her too-bright eyes nearly roll in her sockets as they graze my form. I know what she is looking at is not encouraging. I try to take heart in the fact that I feel the same when looking at her.

"What is your name?" I ask her.

"Rosalind," she says.

"Good evening, Rosalind. Sleep well," I say as I turn away, closing my eyes. A rush of cool, floral scented air tells me she's gone, yet I stay where I am, even as the fire banks itself and the moon rises high into the night. When I finally stir, I prowl silently through the trees, eventually, inevitably, arriving at the river, at the tree where not a day ago I had lain with a girl who held my rose, the rose still hanging over my head. I sit under the tree and let the mist of the silver water wash over me, as sadness and confusion roll in my stomach. Whoever that girl was, is gone. There is now a girl at my castle who is bound to stay, who must be the answer to my predicament. I would do well to forget any romantic notions that I was entertaining about a phantom girl. This is how it is, how it must be, how it will be.

- SIX -
UNKNOWN

I returned to the Wood every day. There was something beyond that beckoned me to enter through the leafy boughs. I snuck out in the spare minutes I have, looped through the trees till I began to form my own paths through the undergrowth to the river. During a day of rain, I constantly looked through the windows at the encroaching trees, as though someone called to me from their shadows. I finally ran out and sat under a sprawling oak, feeling a relief of pressure in my chest as the rain slowly trickled onto my upturned face.

It was a nice relief from the house. Father was weak for days after Rose left, but when he realized there was no one to sit by him as he dwelt on the past, his strength recovered. I thought him healthier than he had been in years. But then he seemed possessed by a nervous energy, forever walking or writing, restless even in sleep. I found myself staring at him as he stood at the window by the fireplace, believing the only thing keeping him there between one blink and the next was my will that he remain.

He went to town one morning, and came back with a job, working with small business accounts in town. He said it was more than time to contribute again, and was always enamored more of numbers than the sums they stood for. He went to town nearly every other day at first light, and always returned before it grew dark. He stoked the fire, no matter how warm the evening is, and placed candles in all the windows facing the Wood. I know he was waiting for her to return, to find her way home by candlelight. But he has grown terrified of the night, of the dark where nothing can be seen until it is too late.

I cannot stand the pulsing flames and dancing lights, though. I often escaped to my room at sunset, sat at the window and watched the night turn the candles from beacons across the grass to tendrils of light.

I find myself skulking through the castle that I've called home for so long, hiding in darkened rooms, listening for footsteps. So many conflicting urges fight within me, and I find that for all my preparations, I'm unprepared. I have my chance before me, and I'm afraid to approach her. All the doubts that had preceded my plan now returned in full force, and it is only her first day here.

Night has always been my ally, but now I have no cover of darkness as I made my way to the dining room. She is not there, but the table is already set, waiting for her. I sit at the right hand of the table, facing the fire and pulling back the heavy curtains. I don't want to hide in the shadows and frighten her more. Nothing is more fearful than the unknown. And yet, there is part of me that wonders if seeing my entire stark image will be more intimidating, leaving nothing to the mercy of darkness. Maybe she'll run.

The smallest of gasps alerts me to her arrival. By the time I look up, though, she is composed, the stillest of statues, her face a flushed heart. I nod to her, and after a moment, she performs a stiff curtsy back, eyes downcast behind her pale hair.

"Will you join me for dinner tonight?" I ask, offering her a choice.

"If you wish it."

"It is at your pleasure whether I remain or not."

She does not reply, perhaps fearing a trap, but she approaches and sits at the head of the table. She serves herself from the dishes, and I observe intently, hoping to divine more about her from her choices of artichoke hearts and chicken breast. She hesitates over her silverware. "You are not...hungry?"

"No, not tonight," I say truthfully.

"Is it tonight?" she says, looking back at the midmorning sun streaming through the tall windows. "I honestly can't tell. I know time has passed since we...since I came here, at least a whole day, but the sun still hasn't set."

"It is a little unnerving," I agree, though there are many more unnerving things here to intimidate her, myself included. "Time works differently here in the Wood. The farther in you get, the more it lingers. An hour stretches out to fill a whole day. Soon it will be high noon sun for a week straight."

"Why do I still know when its time to eat, to sleep?"

"Because you've grown up outside the Wood. Plus, old habits die hard."

She nods slowly, processing as she moves her hands to a pitcher and pours herself a glass of dark red wine. She takes the smallest of sips, but I see her mouth grimace when she swallows.

"Is it not good?" I ask.

"No, that is, I'm sure it is very good. I am unused to wine though. I have never tried it."

"Oh. Well, that pitcher has water, if you'd prefer."

"That's alright, I'll manage," she says. A smile flashes across her face, quickly hidden. Everything about her is contained, restricted, a rose in a greenhouse. I'm unsure whether this is normal for her, or if she is naturally shy. Her looks reflect her attitude; curls securely pinned back, eyes lowered, sleeves long enough to hide her hands. But it all seems on the edge of bursting, of blooming.

"Rose, how old are you?"

"I turned fifteen just this last winter," she says quietly, knife flashing in the firelight as she cuts her food.

"So young..." I whisper to myself, but she hears me.

"Not so young," she corrects, before she remembers who she is speaking to, and freezes over her plate. I nod, and her hands resume their work. "I was supposed to have my first glass of wine on my birthday later this year. But we don't have any to celebrate with, so Father said, when he left for the city, that he would bring some home, but then..." She trails off, and I can't bring myself to ask her to finish. The meal ends in silence, we exchange good evenings, and I leave first this time, retreating outside so she will not fear being followed.

The insistent drive to enter the Wood always brought me to the river. I was loathe to attempt the crossing again, after the disastrous results of before. But day by day, I found myself getting closer to the water, placing hand and foot in, standing in the shallows, perching on the larger rocks, until the day came that I crossed the river with no thought at all. As I stood on the far shore, I felt like singing. Though the Wood by my house was now familiar and refreshing, this unexplored maze of trees matched the unfamiliar terrain of my heart. That day, I simply sat under the tree I had woken up under days ago, but I was already making plans.

I've taken to sleeping in the rose garden. Both sides of myself are unwilling to stay in the castle for long, the man for fear of what the beast might do, and the beast for fear of what now dwells in the castle. As much as it has been a shelter to me, I do not need it. It is a luxury, one I would rather impart on Rose. She tells me each day of new wonders discovered in the castle, things that had not previously existed to my knowledge – a music room, an art gallery, dozens of contained courtyards, complete with fruit trees blooming out of season and swinging seats beneath the branches. I am glad it has a more appreciative guest that it can please and delight. I retreat to the rose garden, ever constant, never changing. Though it is a painful reminder at times, it is too beautiful to hate. Tonight, more than ever, I search the countless windows before me, wondering if any look into her room. At dinner, we have come to the topic of her far past, back when she lived in a splendid house in a large city.

"It's been three years since we left," she says. "Already the details of that life are fading. I was often in my room, content with my books, observing instead of being observed. The glamour of the society my family kept was never truly my realm." Another of her rare smiles crosses her face. "It always seemed so bright, so fast. I was curious, but when I eventually did try to join in...it was not the best time to do so. And soon after, we left." Her attention drops down to her plate, and I wonder at all that she has not said. I wish to know more about her, to hear what she thinks in silence. It is so seldom that I see her, only once a day for dinner, and though she does not fear me more, she does not fear me less either. I could always force her to tell me more. I know the power I hold over her, the same power I held over her father. My mind recoils at the memory of that encounter, though, and I have no desire to make things worse by reminding her of what I can do. But the memory does bring something to mind.

"Your father, he called you Rose."

Another small smile. "You may call me that, if you wish."

"Only if you prefer."

"My father always calls me his little flower, his Rose. I don't mind the nickname." But I have begun to learn a little of her different kinds of stillness. This one spoke of regret and unhappiness.

"Rosalind is just as beautiful, and if I may be bold, it becomes you more." She looks up at that, her eyes wide as if with fear, but she leans in.

"You believe so?"

"Rose is a child's name. Rosalind is a woman's name." I offer a raised eyebrow, wondering if she'll remember our first dinner, and I'm pleased to hear a laugh, the first I've ever heard her utter. It quickly subsides, but the smile lingers until we part ways.

Giselle had begun to pull some weight around the house. Slight though her help was, it was always offered freely, and I enjoyed working along side her, enjoying the companionship that I had been sorely lacking in the past months. She accepted my trips to the Wood, though she did not understand why, nor did she push further the subject of Rose. When I returned home from my successful crossing of the river, I took care of the cleaning, laundry and prepared the next day's food. I promised Giselle I would return early enough to prepare dinner, and in exchange for keeping herself alive and fed, and dissembling about where I was in the unlikely case that Father inquired about my whereabouts, I agreed to go into town with her next week for trading and market day. It wasn't high society, but Giselle longed to escape the solitude of the house as I did. We just found solace in different surroundings. It took a great effort for me to fall asleep that night, and the trees outside my window seemed to shake with anticipation as much as I did.

"Tell me about your sisters," I hear myself say at dinner.

Rosalind looks up, her eyes widen, and I wonder what possessed me to say that. It had been a quiet meal, not exactly comfortable, but not laced with tension either. There is an unspoken rule that Rosalind's family is not up for conversation. "I'm sorry, I shouldn't have asked. I just thought I might get to know a little more about you. You don't have to, of course, I understand completely."

However, Rosalind shakes her head. "No, it's alright. I don't mind it, we can talk about anything you want."

A million questions leap up in earnest, but I force myself to remain calm. "Only what you're willing to share. Your father...he told me he had three daughters."

"Yes, I'm the youngest. Father says that I remind him most of our mother. I was thirteen when she died, but even so I remember very little of her. I remember she was bright, shining, always walking like she was on stage, like every movement was carefully planned. I can't recall her face though. It wasn't that I didn't love her, or that she loved me any less than her other daughters. We were just different." I see now that there is a pain in her face that is as much a part of her as her eyes or nose.

"I think Giselle is most like her. She's a true society woman, even now that we live out here in the countryside. She's witty, terribly clever. She's much older than me, and we never found much common ground to unite us. We don't have what she and Evelyn have, they've always been so close. There may have been a time when we were children that Evelyn and I were close, but ever since I tried to join her debut... well, we don't have the best relationship."

"May I ask, what happened? You've mentioned this before."

"I have, haven't I? It happened so long ago, lasted no more than a minute. It was my sister's sixteenth birthday, a debut - an entrance into society. It's all Evelyn could think about or talk about. I hadn't been very interested when Giselle had her first party, but by the time Evelyn started to prepare...I don't know, I thought it would be a way to connect with her, connect with my entire family. I didn't understand the importance of this night to Evelyn."

She turns inward, lost in memory, and I prepare for her to fade to silence, but she draws another breath and continues. "My mother often bought me dresses, many of which had yet to leave the wardrobe, but that night I pulled one on and went down the staircase. I just wanted to see what it looked like, what my sister had been so anxious for. But, when I reached the doorway, the music was silenced, the guests stopped dancing, everything was frozen. And I saw Evelyn's face. I saw her eyes harden, her face close behind a mask, before Mother and Father whisked me away. I had ruined something that could not be fixed. And things only became worse when my mother died." She falls silent, and as much as I want to know more, I would not push her again. "I am sorry for your grief," I say.

She tries to wave off my apology as she stands. "It is not your fault. I have never told anyone this. It hurts me to think that one mistake can change a life forever."

"How right you are," I say, quietly to myself as she leaves.

My dinners with Rosalind bring my days back into the reality of hours and minutes. I make sure to be seated at the table before she arrives, and do not leave till she has. Though she has become quite calm when speaking to me, opening up a little more each day, any excessive movement on my part causes responding tremors in her body. She is as observant of me as I am of her. I create the same stillness in my body as I do when I hunt. In a way, I still hunt her. The more I can hide, the more she will forget what I am. And I enjoy our conversations. The intricacies of her words, as she sidesteps certain things and expounds in detail others, keep my human side in control as I recall the nuances of speech and tone.

During the day, the animal is master. I let him run free in the Wood, my ramblings and feedings checked only by the constant observations of the sun's position overhead, depending on how close to the border I get. Part of me, the part that still thinks about the other girl who slept beside me, leads me in paths ever closer to the river, but I stay away for days, out of fear and something else, something I won't name.

When I finally return to the river, everything has changed.

The morning dew hadn't yet burned off the grass when I reached the river. I drew up my skirt into a knot on my hip, the hem draped across my knees instead of the ground, exposing my high-laced boots. Only in the safety of the Wood would I dress this way · good breeding runs deep, even in the countryside. The crossing of the river was quick, already familiar beneath my feet, and the deep Wood beckoned with wind like a song. I kept my skirt up, eyeing dense foliage and envisioning hidden thorny creepers, and tightened my bootlaces and the straps of my pack. Nothing remained but to go forward.

At first I doubt my senses, thinking the scent in the air is a memory of that night, of any night when the moon shines. But then I see the bent grass, the barely perceptible footprints. She was here. I follow the trail to the looming trees, and I resist the urge to bolt after it like a hound on a fox's tail. I walk slowly, my head low to the ground to hold onto the trail, as if there was any chance of me losing it. It may as well be holding onto my horns and dragging me through the underbrush.

It lingers, halts haphazardly in the roots of oaks and rocky outcroppings. Large stones permeate this portion of the Wood, as tall as the trees and draped in moss and creepers. The few animals that inhabit the Wood rarely come here, and I can understand their trepidation. The looming stones cast deep shadows, and have the feeling of immense ages past, haunted. I have grown accustomed to the spirits that inhabit the castle, and fear no ghosts. Rather, I find them kindred spirits, remnants of forgotten things, covered by the world. Her scent winds through the tight spaces between the boulders, too small for me, so I scale the rock faces, no surface too slick for my claws. As I near the top, I can see the sun breaking through the green to shine brightly on the stone.

Every turn of my head offered new sights, trees that I could not name winding about each other in a frozen dance, leaves as dense as curtains drawn across the sky, eclipsing the sun. The green twilight of the Wood was enchanting, and exhilarating. Every step reminded me I was in a place where few others have been, maybe completely unexplored. Despite the tightly packed vegetation, there was freedom here.

Then I came upon boulders, giant monoliths set at angles in the ground, some taller than our house had been in the city. Many of the smaller ones leaned against each other, slivers of space between them before they inexorably pressed together and were sealed under nets of moss. I saw an opening, only a few feet wide, but as tall as a cathedral door. I stepped into it, shoulders and elbows grazing against the rock as I slid down the natural corridor. It was longer than it appeared from the outside, and my breathing got deeper, trying to gather more air. But I could see the end already, and pure sunshine beyond. I stepped out from the passageway, taking in the stones that rose up around me and encircled a little meadow, soft green with tiny white flowers that were nearly swallowed up in the grass.

Then a shadow fell across the sun, and the white flowers leapt up in the fading light, shining sweetly as stars. I knelt down to look at them better, running my hands through the blossoms. Then a sharp sound, rock against rock, and I turned in time to see a small stone bounce once more off the boulder and land in the grass behind me. I looked up, curious, and saw that the shadow had not come from a cloud or tree. The sun, cresting the stone behind me, had been eclipsed by a shadowy form, solid black. It moved, twisted, and I saw the sun striking it, but it illuminated nothing. It could be anything.

Then the light glinted on sharp claws, sharper teeth, and it solidified into flesh, muscle and fur, larger than I can grasp, too big to exist. I wanted to scream, to release the terror, but it clung to my bones. I knew it saw me. I knew I had no weapon but a small knife, and that the seconds it would take to dig through my pack and unsheathe it would be my last. I remained crouched in the grass, ready to run if the terror would release me. But the only way out was back the way I came, right under where it stood.

And then it moved. Faster than thought it jumped down, claws raking against the stone until it landed before me, blocking off my exit. It towered above me, eclipsing the sun, and in the back of my mind, the dragon handler's words rung clear as if he were right beside me.

Do not look the beast in the eye.

I tried to lower my eyes.

Rest your gaze on the thrashing tail, the glinting claws, but give the face only the briefest of sweeping glances.

I couldn't even blink.

If you linger in its gaze, you may be lost. It will assume all control, and you will not be able to run, even when the danger is already upon you!

I wanted to look away, if only to not see when it finally attacked, but I couldn't. There was no way to escape its gaze, those eyes…the dragon had not had eyes like these.

I had no intention of letting her see me. The pebbles I'd knocked with my paw had been an accident. I'd let my attention slide. But then she looks up at me. Just as I couldn't leave her at the river, I cannot leave her now. Quickly I make my way down into the clearing, needing to make sure, as if I could doubt what all my senses are screaming at me. Those eyes, familiar and foreign, in a shade of grey that is intense enough to almost be a color, do not turn away. Rosalind does not look in my eyes. Neither did her father. But this girl matches my stare, even as her breathing escalates and nervous tremors run up her legs. I take another step closer, forgetting what I am, forgetting I am terrible and wild. I just want to take all of her in and know this is not a dream.

My mind was starting to go blank. Any thoughts of escape
or fight drained out of me. I could only give up and hope that
it was not hungry, that it was not vicious, throw myself on the
good mercies that let me survive the river. Even as it came
closer, I noticed a soft wind whispering through the grass and
the little white flowers that continued to shine in the
darkening shadow. The Wood went on around me. Life went
on, and I was still breathing. The creature stood close enough
that I could touch it with an outstretched hand, impossibly
large and impossibly dark. And then, it sank, lowered itself to
the ground, its gaze level with mine. No longer eclipsed, the
sun shone down on my face and I inhaled deeply, instinctively.
I breathed in warmth, and grass, and the scent of the
creature, animal, yet light and clear, like water. My gaze,
though still alert, softened, and I allowed myself to take the
rest of him in.

He still seemed to take up half the clearing, and the
bright sunlight only intensified the blackness of his fur. Was it
the immensity, the coloring, the fear, that made me think him
male? His back looked as broad as a horse, even larger, and
when the wind came by, it stirred longer hairs along his spine
that looked like a mane. In the paws, I could see the glints of
silver claws. Looking at those too long made my heart start
thumping erratically, though, and I looked back up at the
head, the perked ears and two silver horns jutting up behind
them.

I lay down in a futile attempt to make myself smaller, less
imposing, but it seems to help as she takes a deep breath. Her eyes
start to wander over me, and she slowly shifts her weight off her feet
until she is kneeling in the grass. The clearing is bathed in warm white
light. It would be peaceful if our two hearts weren't pounding loudly in
our chests. But I have no desire to leave. I should want to run, I should
have never followed her. But I'm compelled to follow her, beyond
restraint or thought, by instinct. And that terrifies me.

He shifted, breathed, seemingly ignoring me. But his gaze
continued to flicker back to me, and those eyes…it felt like I'd
been looking at them for hours, yet I still could not place what
made them so strange, so uncanny. The only thing I could say
for certain about them was that they were grey, the grey of an
approaching storm.

He could be domesticated, the familiar of some warlock,
for surely I'd never seen anything like him. But he felt wild, as

easy to tell as the difference between a dog and a wolf. And he clearly hunted, or those claws would be unnecessary. Yet he continued to sit, making no move towards me, or away. My mind still spun around, searching for answers, and the thought struck me that if this were a fox, or a robin, I would not mind it staying a while, sharing the same space. And he was so big, so monumental that it was possible he saw me as I would see the robin. Amidst my fear the briefest of smiles flashed across my face.

She smiled. My gaze returns to hers in full force. Her face doesn't show any indication of happiness, yet I know she smiled. In that smile was a soft reminder of her humanity that I no longer share. I stand slowly. Her face follows mine, her form cast in shadow, and I take in the sight of her hair, her hands, her face framed in the white pinpricks of flowers. And then I leap over her, back up the rocks and away.

The breath left my body as he hovered above me again, details lost but for those eyes. Then he jumped, and by the time I turn around, all I see is the tip of a dark tail as it disappeared behind rock. For another moment I was still, then I collapse in the grass, mind and body spent.

Beyond luck, this was a miracle. He must have been just as surprised as I was to meet another creature in the Wood. And what a creature. Even if I had met the dragon outside its bars, I doubt I would have been as shaken as I had been with this creature. It was like nothing I knew, nothing I could name. It's humanity's nature to name the unnamable. Had not Adam's first task been to name every living thing in God's new world?

Leaning against the warm stone, I could still see the indentations where we had sat, eyes locked. I was surprised to see the sun still high, and made my way back through the rock chasm to the Wood. I half expected to see the creature waiting for me, and there is a part of me that is disappointed by his absence. The encounter had been terrifying, but despite my fear, had there not been a moment right before his departure that there had been a feeling of longing, of a desire to remain in the clearing? And had it come from him, or myself?

I walked home in a daze. Giselle raised an eyebrow at my silent return, but offered no comment. Perhaps she could see the distress in my face, which I clearly felt as I climbed the stairs and collapsed on my bed. I would rise in a while, wash my face, go downstairs and help Giselle make dinner as I had promised. But for now, I slept.

I woke in a haze, the sunlight in the room confusing me. My dreams were dark, filled with water and stars and blue roses. The door opened, and I turned to see Giselle peeking in. "Are you alright? You've been asleep for a few hours." She came in and sat down beside me. "It's almost dinnertime."

"And you managed not to burn down the house in my absence? I'm impressed."

She flashed me a smug look. "I'm not completely incompetent, just morally against exertion. Now tell me what happened."

"What happened where?"

"You know exactly what I mean. You take off at dawn on some mysterious wilderness journey, and return before the sun is even high, looking like you were chased by ghosts."

"No ghosts," I joked, sitting up to meet her calculating gaze and set jaw. She would not leave it at that, and I sighed. "I went to the Wood, down by the river. I walked along the bank for a little while." Very little, and not the bank she would think of. "And then...I thought I saw something, and it scared me, so I came back."

She nodded slowly, seeming to accept my story, but I knew her too well, knew what the little furrow between her eyebrows means, and waited for the further questions. I was not disappointed. "Your boots were wet when you came back."

"There was still a lot of dew in the undergrowth. And, I slipped on the bank a little."

"Is that why your skirt is tied at your knees?"

I looked down, and was shocked to see my shins. I pick at the knot and released the crinkled cloth. "I didn't want the hem to get wet."

"In the river."

"Yes."

"That you accidentally slipped into."

"Yes." I have nothing left but to be stubborn. She has me, and we both know it. But she doesn't go for the kill. The little furrow between her eyebrows vanishes, and a small smile of knowing appears on her face. It appeared the questioning was done, for now. She stood up and pulled me up with her.

"Come on. You can set the table while I finish dinner."

"You actually made dinner?"

"Don't sound so incredulous," she admonished me as she threw an arm around my shoulder. "You wound me to the quick."

Fool. Every choice I have made, from the moment I pulled her from the river, has been the wrong one. As if I'd had a choice then, or now. Of course I had to save her, of course I had to linger to make sure she survived the night, of course I had to touch her and entertain the thoughts that spurred me to rebellious hope. This was not the way it was supposed to be, not the way to my salvation, and yet I had chosen to finally confront her, let her see me as I truly was.

And she had not run...

Of course she hadn't run, she'd been paralyzed with fear.

And then she had smiled...

No she hadn't, she couldn't have, I imagined it.

With surprise I notice the castle looming above me. The sun still hangs high, shadows clinging to the walls, and I cling to these, reminding myself where I belong. For the first time in a long while, I shiver. The sensation remains with me throughout dinner in front of a roaring fire, with Rosalind eyeing me carefully, on edge at my silence. I apologize and leave before she is done. I retreat to my room, but the dark blue rose sits on the floor, impossible to ignore. I loop it back onto my horn again, liking the soft weight on my head. If I hadn't been insane before, I can feel myself starting to turn that way now. The air hangs heavy, and I run back downstairs and escape outside, unconsciously arriving at the river. I curl up in the branches of the massive oak where I can see the night sky, and attempt to sleep.

SEVEN

BREAKTHROUGHS

I woke up at my normal time, did the household chores, sat and ate breakfast quietly. I was trying to return to my life. Nothing had changed, so it should have been simple. But as the afternoon rolled around and I found myself sweeping the floor for the third time, the quiet voice that had been whispering in the back of mind made its presence known. Go, it urged simply. And I wanted to. I went up to my room to tell Giselle that I was leaving, but as I walked past the kitchen, I stopped to see Giselle stoking the fire, hair pulled back and my apron around her waist. Before she could turn around, I snuck up behind and put my arms around her.

She laughed and turned around to kiss my head. "Go on, little Evelyn."

"You can manage the house yourself?"

"Of course. I may not have your unyielding resilience at completing a task, but I can do what needs to be done. Besides, I haven't watched you work for so long without picking up a few tricks." She put the back of her hand on my cheek. "Just be safe. You are my little sister, after all." She tweaked my nose with flour-dusted fingers, and I twisted out of her grasp and ran for the door.

She is here.

I was sure I had scared her away, for days at least, if not forever. But I lift my head, avoiding the beams of morning sunlight, and there she is on the other side of the river, already bunching her skirt at her knees. She makes her way swiftly across, confident in her steps. She lands on the bank beneath me, and if I weren't already frozen, I'm now as still as stone. With only a moment's hesitation, she presses forward, and is soon out of sight in the undergrowth.

I try to remember my choices, that I could stay, or go the other way. But even as I debate, I'm already moving through the treetops, following her scent, as tangible as a thread pulling me along the branches. I guess there never was a choice.

As soon as I stepped beneath the trees, happiness flooded me, brought on by nothing more than the light peeking through the shifting leaves. I felt no dread but rather excitement · who knew what wonders I might see that day? It seemed that the locals were wrong about the lack of living creatures in the Wood. Beyond that, the Wood itself was alive, itself. The wind spilled through the canopy, sending the leaves dancing in the light, down the tiny strands of creek whispering through the moss and ferns. Even the sunlight coming through the trees had a sound. I stood in a beam of light and closed my eyes, face uplifted, to hear it better.

Even with my eyes closed, I felt the shadow cross over. My eyes flashed open, but the light made me close them again as I stepped out of the sun. My mind immediately turned to a figure larger than the sun, black as night. There was something in that flicker of shadow overhead that, beyond recent memory, made me believe that he is there. As before, there was no hope for weaponry defense. I had not even brought a pack today. But I did have the advantage of knowing where he was. I kept walking, slowly, listening for footsteps other than my own. I heard and saw nothing unusual as the minutes passed, and I could almost dismiss my caution, but the sense that I was being followed remained.

In the distance, I could make out a tree, a tree larger than any I've ever seen before. The trunk alone could swallow our old city house with room to spare, and the branches reached out far enough to shade a town. It only got more magnificent the closer I got, till I was at the sprawling red-brown roots, the smallest of which were still as wide as roads. I looked back at the smaller trees, which trailed off in the shadow of this giant, but saw no sign of my supposed follower. I jumped onto a root, arms outstretched to keep my balance as I trekked up towards the trunk.

I expected the slight creak behind me, the whisper of a few falling leaves, but my heart still stumbled. The knowledge of my pursuit was only half the battle. I tried to focus on walking, but as the root got increasingly wider till four of me could comfortably skip across it, hand in hand, my mind wandered to what could be following above. It was a little like fear, the feeling in my chest, but it was more anticipation, lung-stifling anxiety for what was about to happen. I didn't know what would happen, and therein lay the feeling like fear.

The trunk rose up before me in a tangle of segmented roots and vines, more like smoke than wood under the dappled light of a million leaves rustling in unfelt breezes. Large gaps erupted in the russet wood, dark canyons that seemed impenetrable until I was right upon them, and then I saw the small white flowers, illuminating the wooden caves with stolen starlight. They seemed to prefer the low dark places where they could shine more brightly, clustered together like constellations. I wanted to stop and look closer, but I had run out of tree that was flat enough to walk on, and another falling leaf reminded me of my current situation. I found a plateau of wood relatively lit from the filtered sunlight, and when I sat down, it pleasantly warmed the palms of my hands and my calves as I curled my legs underneath me. It took great effort to remain still, to appear calm, as if I was prepared for what could happen.

I was not kept waiting for long. Even with my wary eyes, I did not see him until he was a stone's throw away. And he was fast, leaping from branch to branch with no hesitation. With the immensity of the tree around us, he appeared an almost acceptable size, but then he glided to a halt on a branch above me, so close I could hear his claws dig into the wood, and he filled up my vision like a threatening storm cloud. I willed myself to breathe slowly and deeply, to accept what is happening and continue living. He paused, head lowered in a gesture that would be timidity in any other creature, and I returned to the hope that he was as unsure of me as I was of him. Instinctively I wanted to hold my hand out to him as I would to a skittish horse or wary bird, but his wildness kept my hands clasped together.

Sinuous as silk, he dropped from the branch onto the roots before me. The dappled sunlight did not leaven his dark immensity, but he no longer filled my field of vision, and I was again aware of the tree surrounding us, of the warm wood beneath my knees. He did not sit, but slowly paced back and forth, looking everywhere but at me. When he finally did look towards me, he shook his head and snorted. It sounded like a dog when it has a scent it can't get out of its nose, and I couldn't help it, I laughed. His gaze darted back to me, eyes wide with what I can only translate as shock, and I stifled my laugh, but continued to smile. He sat back on his haunches with his eyes still fixed on me. The more I looked, the more animals I saw in him - wolf, horse, lion, dragon. I still could not place his eyes though.

Emboldened, and perhaps unable to contain my nervous energy, I stood up and slowly, purposefully, walked towards him. I couldn't avoid the Wood, and it appeared I couldn't avoid him, so I'd rather know now what would become of me. We were face-to-face, so close I could see the individual strands of glinting fur. I could see myself reflected in those unfathomable grey eyes. I felt my resolve weakening, his strangeness too unnerving to bear, the fear of the unknown hanging in my chest. As much as I wished to have whatever was going to happen done with, I was reminded of the fact that I was not quite ready for death. I nearly gasped for air, and then a breeze, the first I've felt in the shade of this tree, sneaked by us and brought his scent to me. Animal, yet light and clear, like water, and with it came the memory of our first meeting, and a time before that, a cold and clear night, with the roar of a river that had leapt up to consume me, and then…a warmth in the night, leaving behind only long black hairs in the morning. His head moved infinitesimally, and something dark fell, settled at the base of one of his horns - a cloth rose, midnight blue.

"You have my rose," I said aloud. "How do you…the last I saw it was at the river," I slowly worked through the recognition dawning in my mind. "You pulled me from the river. You saved me."

Was it too much to hope she would not make the connection? But I know that I only encouraged her to discover the truth by finding her and following her, showing myself to her, keeping her rose with me. Every one of these acts reprehensible, reckless, dangerous… thrilling. Now that I've heard her voice, not a scream or a laugh but actual words, I know it will haunt my dreams. Before I can think of reacting, of answering, she speaks again.

"Yes, I'm sure it was you, it must be you, there's nothing else that lives here, not that I have seen, but…a creature such as you, surely there would have been stories. Maybe, you haven't always been here?" How closely she walks around the truth, but she does not wait for my acknowledgment. "I would wonder why you are following me, but I am doing the same thing, aren't I? Tracking is one thing, following quite another, so I do not dare call you an animal, you are clearly something altogether different, as different as a bloodhound is from a wolf, only…not at all like that. I'm not sure what, exactly, not that it matters, I'm really just rambling now in hopes that you will not decide to eat me."

Her words are serious, but the tone is light, calm, and she has not moved, nor does she seem inclined to think I will respond. I am still debating whether speaking now will help or hurt matters. I don't want her to think of me as an animal, though. It would be easy to feign wildness, just run away now and attempt to forget her, despite my lack of previous success in that area, but I foolishly want her to know I am more.

She continues, "Our previous encounters seems to indicate you would rather not eat me, but I've been wrong before. It is very likely I've imagined this spirit of camaraderie between us, and you are lulling me into false security. I do not think I am worth this much effort, frankly, but then I've never tasted girl, so my opinion is limited. In any case, it matters little whether you can understand me or not." She takes a shuddering breath, the only sign of her distress, and I am reminded of what I am. But she continues, "At the moment, I would most like to know where we stand with each other."

This I can answer easily. I stand up and execute the most courtly bow I can muster in this form, front half sinking low to the earth, one paw bent beneath my lowered head. When I rise, her eyes are wide in astonishment, but after a long moment, she lowers herself into a curtsey. "Now we have met properly," she declares solemnly, then breaks down with a little laugh. "Truth be told, I am glad we understand a little of each other. I've grown weary of talking to walls."

It would no doubt seem strange to me later, but at the moment, standing in the Wood with this sapient beast seemed, if not comfortable, at least preferable to life back home. Not for the first time, I wondered why the Wood held such sway over me, I who never felt a thing for trees or grass or dirt before we moved here. He continued to stare at me, unnerving but not intrusive. I decided to test our understanding.

"So, you know I do not live in the Wood. Do you live here?"

A deliberate nod. I found myself inordinately pleased.

"Have you always lived here?"

This time a shake of his head, like a horse shaking off dust.

"Neither have I. I used to live in a large, grand city," I explained, finding myself using my hands as visual aids to convey the description of my old life. "Buildings as tall as trees. Well," I corrected with a laugh and a gesturing hand, "none as tall as *this* tree. Where did you live before?"

A stillness overcame him, and my happiness caught in my throat. His eyes drifted from mine, off into the distance, but I sensed what he was seeing was inside himself. Then he blinked, shoulders shuddering as if he's settling into his skin, and I did not ask him again. I turned to the tree again. "It's so grand, it must be hundreds of years old, but it doesn't feel old, it feels...alive."

He nodded his head, then lowered himself to the root beneath us and laid the side of his head on the wood, eyes still looking up at me. I slowly knelt too, placed my hands on the root and cautiously lowered my ear to the wood. It was quiet, and then, so low that I could feel it in the palms of my hands, a thump deep in the wood. My eyes darted to him, where he remained motionless but for his eyes, which flicked down to the wood and back up to me. I continued to listen, and it sounded again, a reverberation like the string of a harp. In recognition I exclaimed, "It sounds like a heart beating!"

He lifted his head to nod, but I remained where I was, listening to the heartbeat of a tree too impossibly big to exist. I glanced up at him, and remembered that it wasn't so strange to find the impossible, possible, here. He lowered his head again, resting his chin on crossed paws, and the image was so close to the cats in town resting on the windowsills that I laughed. I'd laughed more freely in his company than ever before, without having to wait for appropriate pauses in a witty conversation, or maintain a respectable volume. Here I could touch the grass with my bare feet, I could laugh loudly. I could have a conversation with a creature who I had previously thought had intentions of eating me, and there was no one to tell me to feel any other way than I did.

In the shade, I had no idea of how long we had sat here, the time all melded into dappled sunlight, words and silence and beating hearts. He was still seated before me, still strange and impossible, but no longer unfamiliar. Involuntarily I got to my feet. I knew I should be getting home, but, now more than ever, I found myself reluctant to leave the Wood. "I don't even know how to get back to the river from here," I said quietly to myself, but then he rose, fluid and dark, and walked ahead of me down the trunk. He paused, turned as if to make sure I'm following, and led me back, winding through trees and undergrowth without a sound. As we walked, when I could tear my gaze away from him, I noticed that certain russet roots I would have previously thought belonged to nearby trees, were suddenly clear as extensions of the impossibly large tree, the tree with a heartbeat. Even if I couldn't see them, I could feel faint vibrations in my feet when I stood in one place for a moment. When I paused, he paused, watching each other intently. By the time we reached the river, the last rays of daylight had set it ablaze. "Thank you," I told him as I tied up my skirt, suddenly afraid of meeting his gaze. The normalcy of life back over the river rushed to claim me, and made me brisk, polite, distant. But he was impossible to ignore, and so I did turn to meet his gaze, his unnerving eyes. A small piece of the happiness from this afternoon resurfaced in my mind, and this urged me to say, "Will I see you again?"

He held my gaze a moment longer, then extended his paw, the glistening golden claws and pawed at his head, severing the rose from his horn. It fell to the ground, and he pushed it to my feet. He then scratched slowly, carefully in the dirt, and stepped back. I knelt down and saw, jagged but clear letters in the soil – *yes*. I raised my head, but he was already gone.

She overwhelms my senses as I fly through the trees. The rush of hearing her voice, the little nuances in her eyebrows and lips, and her scent, dizzying. The longer I remain with her, the more I realize the truth of us, and the less I care. She is human, I am no longer, and yet there is none of the agony for our differences as there is with Rosalind. Instead of feeling trapped, I feel free. I hadn't even known this body of mine could write human words still. I had never tried it. Of course, this girl knows none of that. She doesn't even know I can speak. Better for her to think me animal, intelligent, trained, but not human. No longer human.

I wind my way through the garden, still lost in thought, when a bright glare strikes my eye, and I look up to see a window opening far off in the broad face of the castle. I see Rosalind's head and shoulders lean out to the ledge. I quickly retreat into shadow, but she is staring beyond me, at the Wood. At that height, she can only see tree trunks and thick canopies, but she continues to look, entranced by it. Her hair hangs freely in the breeze, a light shawl wrapped around her shoulders. So this is where her room is, in the far wing nearest the tree line. I wonder if she is looking for her home, hoping for a glimpse of something familiar through the trees. How often have I run through those trees, searching for the same? This castle, no matter how accommodating it becomes, has never been more than shelter for me. But Rosalind has already turned away, though she leaves the window open as she retreats back into her room. I make my way to the dining room.

Rosalind intrigues me, mainly with her silence. I know I'm not the best company, but she will halt conversations in the middle of words, offering no explanation. At first I thought it fear, and perhaps it still is, but not of me. Things have happened to her that make her afraid to speak her mind too long, too loud. The initial wonder of the castle has worn off, and too many failed attempts at conversation begin to wear at my persistence. If I am honest with myself, I know I am trying less, but I can't seem to find a common ground for us, and the meals grow quieter than the crackle of the fire.

However, tonight, Rosalind places a book on the table beside her. I gaze at the spine, but I can't make out the letters, faded beyond recognition into the worn leather. "Are you enjoying it?"

She pauses with the wine glass at her lips, eyes wide. Then she seems to remember the book beside her and gives a small laugh. "Oh, yes, I am, that's why I brought it with me. One of my old favorites, I came across it this morning, and I've been reading it ever since. I nearly forgot dinner, I only realized because I was hungry, I still can't tell one hour from the next here." Her face, so open and excited, slowly begins to close. "I'm sorry if I was late."

"No, don't apologize," I say, but she is already stiffening, freezing. I fight against it. "This is one of your books, that you brought with you?"

"Yes, it's one of the few books I kept from our time in the city. I used to have a whole wall, full of shelves and shelves of books. We sold most of them to pay the debts, but I managed to keep a few of my favorites. This," she touches the book lovingly, "is a play by Arimanthanes. I've read it too many times to count."

"It certainly looks that way. That's why I asked if it was yours, it didn't look like one of the books from the library."

"What library?"

"The library here. It's just down the hall."

Her eyes, usually wide and still with anxiety, narrow and gleam as she scrutinizes me. "You have a library?"

A grin spreads across my face. "Would you like to see it?"

She stands up and stretches out an arm to the door. "Lead the way."

"Right now?"

"Dinner can wait," she says, practically bouncing. Her enthusiasm is catching, and we nearly sprint down the hall to the double doors of the library. She pulls them open, and I am amazed to see lights already ablaze inside, but am grateful for the impression they'll create for her. I've seen the room before, but watching her halt in amazement at the literal forest of books gives it a new level of wonder. She twirls around the room, hands clasped, her face nearly glowing from her radiant smile. It is the first time I have seen her as something not to be pitied or sheltered - rather, she is as innocent and beautiful as a sunrise. The way she runs her hands along the spines makes my own spine shiver to be touched. I turn to leave, but she runs back to me and looks in my eyes for the first time since the evening we met. "Thank you," she says, and I can only nod before she is off again, already scaling one of the many spiral staircases.

Have I finally broken through to her? Not till now have I seen anything about her captivity bring her any comfort or joy. And she thanked me for it! But I doubt anything has changed. She would much rather have this room than my company. Even now she retreats further and further into the library, a solitary act, and I stand at the door, forgotten. Am I selfish, or jaded? Dinner arrives at one of the reading desks, just enough for her, my signal to leave. Rosalind, distant in the shelves, but bright as a flame, doesn't turn at my departure.

A written word in the dirt, *yes*. So simple, but impossible to ignore. The minute I left the Wood, I longed to return, say yes to all my foolish desires and impossible dreams. I quietly snuck into the candlelit house, into my bed, but sleep did not come to me. My heart beat erratically, blood rushed through my limbs, and after hours of trying to drift to sleep, I went to sit at the windowsill, where I had set my recently returned rose. I turned it over in my hands, marveling again at the resemblance it bore to a real rose. I pulled out from my drawer of scraps a length of silver rope that had once pulled the stays of my ball gown together, and set to sewing the rose to it, like a gem on a chain. The cool night air rushed over my flushed face, the murmuring of the trees seemed a song and the frenetic energy in my body turned to one of quiet determination, as I counted stitches, the stars faded, and the moon slowly slid away before the dawn. At first light, I went to the washbasin, splashed my face and ran my wet fingers through my hair. The sunlight struck a corner of the small mirror on the wall, reflecting onto my face. I saw half of my face hidden in shadow, the other side too bright to make out details, but where my grey eyes should be, silver glinted instead, like water or starlight. I covered my face in the washcloth, dried my skin, and when I looked back into the mirror, the sunlight evenly lit my familiar face. The gleam of silver in my eye was from the metal of the washbasin, nothing more.

The house was quiet, with Father off at work and Giselle still asleep. I returned to my chores, dependable and boring, retrieving water from the well, baking bread that Giselle had set out overnight, shaking the rug, sweeping floor and hearth. It made my already tired muscles ache more, but it was comforting and fulfilling, and unfortunately done all too soon, as the sun was not yet high in the sky as I swept the last of the dirt off the front stone steps. When Giselle eventually came down and asked if we were going to town that day, I jumped at the chance to leave, hoping to forget the events that had happened. There was the slightest twitch in my feet when we passed by the place where I normally entered the Wood, but I remained resolute, and soon we could hear the noise of the town, a cacophony of the cries of livestock and humanity.

Within town, it was easy to pretend we were back in the city. The people rushing past, the tinkling of carts full of trinkets, perhaps a few too many loose chickens, but I could see why Giselle came as often as she could. What little money we had came from Father's odd jobs, so we depended on barter for the rest, using the stolen remnants of our old life, like silk ribbons and seed pearls torn from my bodices, exotic feathers and leathers. I hoped that we'd have more experience in making things of usefulness – herbs, breads, cheese – before the basket ran dry, but when I went though it looking for a suitable trade for a piece of cured ham, I came across a little gold bracelet with green stones that was very familiar. I dug deeper, and my hand struck coins. Many, many coins. Shocked, I pulled one out, and handed it over. There had never been more than a few coins in the basket. I had never asked him for money, and he had never offered, but perhaps…

"Giselle," I remarked as we left town with our purchases, "have you finally decided to chip in?"

"What do you mean?" she said offhand, looking down the road, which was mostly deserted as it wound through the hills. The only other person who lived as far out as us was a garden witch, and I had never seen her use the roads to travel. Perhaps once a month, I saw her on the edges of the Wood, gathering herbs. I always gave her a wide berth, each of us attending to our own personal pursuits.

"I mean there is more in the basket than there was before."

She remained disinterested, so I pressed.

"Including the bracelet Mother gave you for your sixth birthday."

A small smile appeared at the corner of her lips.

"What has gotten into you?"

"Can't a sister contribute to the wellbeing of her family?"

"You can, it's just very…unlike you."

Giselle laughed. "You mean it's not a selfish act."

"I wouldn't say that."

"That's because you're too polite to say so," she teased me. "The bracelet is too small, in any case, and one of the stones fell out."

"And helping around the house?"

"All in the name of image, Evelyn. Can't have the house become a sty in your adventurous absences."

I stared down at my feet, unable to object, but she linked my arm through hers, holding me close to her side. "Not to fear, little Evelyn. It is time for me to assume my duties as eldest of the household."

"And what will become of me then?"

"Well, I still need someone to order about."

I bumped her with my hip. Months of manual labor were on my side as she slipped from my grip and stumbled into a bush. I was unable to stifle my laughter as I pulled her upright, but I did help her pick the pieces of bramble out of her carefully coiffed hair as we continued down the road.

That evening, after I'd cleaned up from dinner, I walked into the living room to see Father standing at the window, candles lit, an all too familiar pose. But I broke the silence this time. "Father, I wanted to thank you."

"For what, Evelyn?" His voice, though soft, did not seem distant.

"For the money. I found it in our barter basket today in town. Business must be going well?" I offered the question as a way to actually talk to him, not at him. But he turned to me with an inquiring look and said, "What money?"

"The money in our basket...there must be over fifty coins," I said as he walked past me, grabbed the basket off the shelf and walked to the kitchen. I entered to see him upending it on the table. Fabric, jewels, feathers, and then coins. So many coins, much more than what I had counted this afternoon. And they kept coming, spilling onto the floor. Father appeared frozen, and I rushed forward to take the basket from his hands and turned it upright again. The last few coins thrummed themselves to silence on the wood, and I examined the inside of the basket to find it completely empty. There was enough money on the table to have filled ten baskets. On a hunch, I turned over the basket again, and was only a little surprised to see more money begin to fall out. I righted the once again empty basket, and looked up to see Giselle in the doorway, mouth open and eyes wide. Father sank slowly into a chair, gazing at the small mountain of coins before him.

"He did say we would be compensated," he said quietly.

"What is happening?" Giselle squeaked out, stiffly coming into the room, coins gently clinking underfoot. "Where did all this come from?"

I looked at Father, waiting for a cue from him. I don't see a way of getting out of this without coming clean with Giselle and telling her the truth about where Rose went. But before Father could speak, Giselle surprised us by saying, "It's for Rose, isn't it?"

"What?" said Father, momentarily thrown.

"It's from that man she ran off to be with, isn't it? The one that helped Father on his trip. A dowry fit for a future duchess, certainly. Won't invite us to the wedding, but at least her fiancée has the decency to remember his new family." She reached down and picked from the pile her green and gold bracelet. "Guess I can take this back then."

I sat the basket on the ground, and Giselle and Father pushed the money across the table to cascade down to the basket in a metallic waterfall, while I gathered the coins that fell on the floor. The basket managed to hold the mountainous pile, but when I picked it up, it weighed as much as if it were empty. I put my hand inside and felt the coins below the fabric and feathers. "Very useful," I muttered to myself.

"We must be careful now," said Father. "We can't spend too much at a time," and he stared pointedly at Giselle, who quickly threw an innocent smile on her face. "We don't want to raise questions." His shoulders were hunched, braced as if his past is knocking at the door to bankrupt him again.

"We'll be careful, Father," I assured him, my arms wrapped tightly around the basket.

"Very careful," echoed Giselle, whom I can already see having dreams about chiffon and emeralds. I placed the basket back on its shelf, but covered it with a shawl. We all headed to our rooms soon after, but Giselle and I sat up as the sun set, discussing what we should do with our newfound fortune, just like the old days when we had first moved here, planning parties and sewing pearls out of thread.

"A dress of silk," said Giselle as she bounced on her bed.

"A stable of horses," I countered from my own bed.

"Banquets!"

"A new house."

"A new life!" Giselle exclaimed. "What if the money never runs out? We could move back to the city, get an even bigger house than before, return to society." She looked at me with joyful eyes, but I couldn't match her enthusiasm, and she noticed. "Don't you want to go back to the way things were?"

"I guess so…"

"You guess so?"

"Well, yes, in some ways, I wish we could go back. But I don't think any amount of money will make things the way they were."

"Exactly! It would be better than before! The finer things in life would be ours again, and no man would be able to resist us." She cast a knowing glance at me. "Or do you already have a man?"

I gave her a sardonic look that she would be sure to see even by candlelight.

"Alright, alright. So, what do you want? Say it, and now it can be yours!"

What do I want? The words rang in my head as I lay awake, unable to fall asleep and dream like Giselle. Wealth, fame, men. These were things that were easy to want, ingrained by my mother, woman of society and light of the party. But was that what I hoped for, what I wished would happen? What did I want?

EIGHT

CONFRONTATIONS

The next day at dinner, I encourage the conversation between Rosalind and myself. I ask her about the library, what books and authors she likes, how she spends her days her and what more she requires to be happy. And, miraculously, she responds. Her face lights up as she discusses her favorite authors, her often failed attempts to write poetry, the art room where she spends some days dabbling in the paints and inks, and even a few timid requests, like tea and honey in the late afternoons, or a dressing gown for early mornings. Already I know more about her than I had uncovered in weeks of attempted conversation, and every night she continues to open up, forgetting the stifled terror that used to fill her whenever she remembered my presence. I stay away from the river, and only go outside when absolutely necessary to feed my animal side and keep it sated. I spend my days planning, arranging things to spark Rosalind's interest if she happens to pass by them. I am careful to not let her see me, studying to see what she appreciates most so I can replicate it.

I learn that her sixteenth birthday is only a few weeks away. I remember her story of her sisters' debut at that age, the importance of it, and a thought begins to grow in my mind – a surprise celebration for Rosalind. Her favorite things, foods, books, all for her. Then she would see how I care for her, and that she could care for me. Little by little, I assemble the pieces to bring this party to life, and then, the day of her birthday arrives.

As usual, I stay out of her sight, but I know exactly how her day will progress. She'll wake up to a breakfast of powdered cakes and hot chocolate, her guilty pleasure. When she gets out of bed, a beautiful silk dressing gown will be waiting for her, along with a group of jeweled music boxes shaped like birds of paradise that sing when you open their hinged beaks. I know she prefers her own clothes to the bejeweled gowns in her closet, so I've given her accessories instead – combs for her hair, scarves and shawls, soft shoes and ribbons - all simple, but tasteful, with nothing to outshine her natural beauty. She spends most of her mornings reading what books she brought back with her on the balcony. However, when she leaves her room, on the floor in front of her doors is the end of a golden string leading down the hall. For all the amazing items the spirits here have managed to produce from my halting explanations, intelligible writing is one thing they cannot achieve, and my own experiments in dipping my claws in ink have proved disastrous for the paper and whatever it was sitting on. However, this is just as effective as an instructional map, and I hope she will get the ironic comparison to Adriadne's thread in the Minotaur's maze. Following it down the hall will lead her to the art room, where I have carefully arranged several still life arrangements of flowers, vases and fruits for her to choose from and enjoy. Lunch will be brought to her, a plate of breads, cheeses and spreads to snack on while she paints. In the late afternoon, I slink to the art room and see her seated in front of my favorite arrangement, full of orchids and blood oranges in golden goblets, the hot colors etched in my human memories. As for metals, the distinction between silver and gold is one of the few comparisons I can still accurately detect. Gold is warmer, softer, but silver is brighter.

Dinner finally arrives, and I head to the library, which is decorated as I had hoped, with golden candles, great bunches of golden silks adorning the windows and banisters, vases overflowing with flowers, and a dinner for two set in the middle of the recently shined marble floor. Nothing much can be done for me, but I groomed as best I could, and shined my horns against a taut strip of cloth that I wrapped between my two front paws. I stand on the second floor where I can watch her come in. It is not lost on me that, no matter how I push the animal away, he is always there in the motionless way I wait for her, like prey crossing my path. But this time I rationalize it away.

Courting is a hunt, familiar territory. I had done it before. Second son of a king and queen who had a country to rule and an eldest son to raise to carry on their legacy after they had gone, I learned about love through tales and legends, grand acts of valor and the intimate whispers exchanged between lovers in the dead of night. When, as custom, I was betrothed to a girl in a neighboring kingdom, I knew the responsibilities of such a promise and took every opportunity to learn more about her, whether through visiting emissaries, corresponding to her through letters, or when she would come to visit twice a year. It was not long till I knew everything that could be written down about her, and with every interaction, I strived to show her my devotion and the ways in which I would be a fit husband for her. She was easy to love - beautiful, bright and slender, with a smile both reward and encouragement.

In the week before our wedding, I took my intended on a trip across our kingdoms, the longest we'd spent in each other's company since we were first engaged. On the third day of our trip, halted for the evening in the fields outside the Wood, I stated my feelings plain, without need of ceremony. Surely she must know that throughout all these years, I had grown to love her dearly, could not imagine a life without her. She was guileless, and so she told me that she did not love me, at least not as I loved her. She saw our future, and had accepted it fully, along with all its inherent responsibilities. But she did not yearn for it as I did. She had no reservations that our relationship would hold strong, for she had made herself strong to accept this task of union as a load to bear on her shoulders. Certainly I was sweet and kind, as she was sweet and kind to me, and maybe one day, out of that would grow a love as strong as the bonds of duty that yoked her to me. But now, only days from our wedding, surely I must feel the same as she, that this was an alliance, nothing more.

I was young, and could not hold back the hurt and anger at her revelation. I had never seen her cry before, and I was loath to be the one to bring it upon her, but there was no one else to direct my betrayal at. She tried to calm me, explain her side, but nothing tempered my rage, for I had spent the last several years of my life wooing the woman who was to be my wife, who saw our impending marriage not as a celebration of love, but an enacting of protocol. I wanted to run, run far away from this pain and never experience it again. I promised to her that if we did get married, we would both grow to regret it.

For all the things I knew about my fiancée, I was up to this point entirely unaware of the strain of ancient magic that ran through her family tree, and the training she had received to mold and guide it, to enact it in times of need and use it to teach, to grow. That all changed as she raised her arms, and I saw her fingertips glow like starlight, weaving symbols through the air that wrapped around me like water. I heard her words through the roaring in my ears...

"How dare you hurt me under the pretense of love! You are under the belief that love and duty are two separate things. They are not. I can grow to love you out of duty, but you are set against honoring duty through your love. You have hurt me, it is true, but then, I have also hurt you. So, I set you free to find your own love, free from the bonds of humanity."

Images flashed before my eyes, dark trees, a castle, a garden full of roses, but the color began to leech away till everything was shrouded in grey. "You will remain disguised and lost until another learns to love you, as you love her, truly, so that you bind yourself to her, forever.

"You will have all you need, as long as it takes. The roses will bring you together." A brief pressure on my forehead – her lips? – and then her final words to me. "Please know, I never meant you any pain." And then I blacked out.

When I came to, she was gone, and I was as I have been for innumerable years. It took great effort to convinced the frightened livery that had accompanied us on this trip that I was who I said I was, due in no small part to the unfamiliar mechanisms of my new mouth, as well as their lingering terror. By the time everything had been sorted out, my fiancée and her entourage had disappeared, and any thoughts I may have had about chasing her down were eclipsed by new feelings, new hungers. I ate the meat we had brought for the rest of the week in one sitting, slept till daybreak, and then we made the journey back.

I hid in the wagons to get back into the city, my new senses urging caution and fear around so many people, and snuck into my room in the dead of night by scaling the castle walls, ludicrously easy in this body. I wanted to hide forever, and previously I could have gone unnoticed by my parents for weeks, but my impending wedding made me a now unwanted center of attention, and, after barricading the door against a veritable army of attendants, even they had to leave their meetings to see what had become of me.

When my father first saw me, he froze, one hand on the doorframe. It was the first I ever saw him flustered. My father, who knew how to rouse armies and calm diplomats, was stymied when faced with my transformation. My mother came in after him and with a small cry, stumbled, and I thought she might fall. I took a step toward her to help. My father seemed to awake at my movement, and reached out to help my mother steady herself, placing himself between us, perhaps unconsciously shielding her from attack. After I had told my story, my father wanted to launch a war with my betrothed's country, but even as my mother, the voice of reason, implored him not to for several reasons, not least of which was her country's unknown magical prowess against mere physical strength, I knew it would lead to naught.

A day and a night was spent debating with my intended's mother, queen of her own land and her royal emissaries, who had traveled to attend the wedding, on how best to handle the situation. On the day before I was supposed to be wed, my parents held court with those families who had been invited to the celebration.

In so many eloquent words crafted by our best wordsmiths, the wedding was called off, and the gathered court was told an altered version of the incident which led to my transformation, in which a passing sorcerer kidnapped my betrothed, and cursed me in kind. The story was worded in such a way that there could be no blame placed on either country, nor suspicion cast on the magical powers of the visiting kingdom's royal family. There were a few who tittered in disbelief, but then I appeared from behind a curtained column, and the stifled screams assured us our story was believed. Looking at the assembled in varying shades of grey, I could practically taste their fear as I calmly spoke to them, assuring them that what had been said was true. I wanted to tell them not to fear me, that I was still their prince, but I knew it wasn't true, and instead stuck to the words they had told me to say, encouraging unity and support between our two kingdoms, and when I told them to pray for the princess's recovery, it sounded strained only to my ears. As agreed upon, whenever the princess returned home, it would be said in her kingdom that she had escaped the sorcerer, and upon finding me as I was, I thought it only kind to release her from our engagement so she could have a normal life.

Thus, my engagement was ended, and to every eligible woman gathered there that day, it was subtly implied that they had an opportunity that had not previously existed in our country. Unable to return to my human self until I could love and be loved, I had no choice but to entertain every woman that came to the castle door with every intention of lifting my curse. Over a fine dinner, I would attempt courtly conversation with women ranging from the mutely terrified to the disingenuous flirts. A prince was a prince, after all, no matter what he looked like, and those women viewed me as an investment toward a better life. I found myself inherently more curious in the girls who were frightened, who sat with me while fear swept through their bodies. What inner courage did they possess to have dinner with a monster? Regardless, none loved me. Or if they did, I didn't love them. We were fighting an uphill battle. A line began to form in front of the castle. When I would step onto my balcony, stifled as I was indoors, they would all gasp, half in terror, half with enthusiasm.

As months passed, I began to give up my courtly pretenses and let my silence build into a presence all its own in the dining room. Not just the women, but the servants and courtiers too, everyone gave me a wide berth as I prowled the hallways. I was constantly hungry, no matter how much I ate, and even my mother and father could not give me any comfort, so sure were they that the curse would be lifted soon. I thought often of my elder brother, gone on missions of peace and exploration for the good of the kingdom, who still had not seen, and had not been told, what I had become. He wrote letters to us often, not just about the status of his diplomatic mission, but personal messages to each of us. Preparing since he was born to be king, he and I were no closer than I was with my parents, but still we had familiarities, grounded in no more than the bond of brotherhood. He always had a story to share, or advice to give that came from friendship, rather than age or ranking. His letters became bright spots in my day, a glimpse of a world I had yet to see. To say they gave me hope would be woefully inadequate, but they did give me determination. I would hold onto my humanity, and though cursed, I would not give up.

Then came the day that we received word – the princess' retinue had returned, haggard from hardship and unable to say where the princess had gone since that fateful night. They had gotten separated in The Wood, and every attempt to recover her had brought only more difficulties as the trees themselves seemed to conspire against them. When they finally emerged from its depths, they had little they were willing to share about their experiences, other than their regret at the loss of the princess.

Late that night, I jumped from my balcony, my body instinctively guiding me from outcropping to ledge until I hit the ground and started running. There was no plan, no path, just away, away from what my life had become. I had succumbed to my fate, animal forever.

And if I came across her in The Wood, so be it.

In moments, my past life washed away beneath my new animal senses, alive in the dark after months of repression. By the time I reached The Wood, my humanity had hidden itself away. That night was the first I tasted blood, raw flesh and sinew, my first kill. I don't know how long I remained in this fugue state. I only knew when to run, when to sleep, when to hunt. It could have been years.

And then, one day, I found the roses.

Something moves, and I emerge from my reminiscence and look down to see the arrival of Rosalind, hesitant, yet hopeful in her pause at the open door. She has many evening gowns to choose from, but she's chosen one that sparkles warmly in the candlelight and flares out like a flower, like she instinctively knew which would match her surprise the most. I watch her take in the decorated library with a wondering smile, and when I move down the steps towards her, she doesn't start with fear, but surprise.

"What is all this?"

"Your birthday celebration."

"My birthday? Then... the breakfast, the shoes and ribbons, the flowers..."

"All presents for your celebration. Did you like them?"

"They were all so lovely," she exclaimed, hands clasped. "I enjoyed the music boxes so much, I left them open all morning, and I never had to wind them up." She looked towards the table set for two. "Is this why the dining hall was dark?"

"This is your favorite room," I said as I stepped off the stairs. "I thought you'd enjoy dinner here the most."

"I would, for although I've never eaten in a library, I've eaten with a book many a time." She laughs and sits herself down at the table, possessed with rare confidence. It increases my hope, and I seat myself at the other end.

Dinner flies by in bright whirlwind of conversation and wine. My glass is under the table at my feet, and I only lap at it when Rosalind isn't looking. My animal side doesn't much care for the taste or the effects, but it reminds me of my humanity, and keeps me focused on the task at hand. Rosalind pours herself her second glass as her plate is filled with desserts.

"Back in our old life, the wine at your sixteenth birthday was very important. Father would bring up a cask of wine with a colorful back story, something recovered on one of his trading voyages and saved for this special occasion." She sips deeply. "I know I'm not usually one for wine, but tonight, I feel like celebrating."

"Have you enjoyed your birthday?"

"Very much so," she exclaims, smile radiant. "I can't imagine a more perfect evening."

This is it, the moment. I stand up, ask her to follow me, and I lead her out, down the hall and front stairs, out into the starlight. Outside are hanging lanterns, candles burning low in their globes. I give a little growl, and the flames flare up in attention, illuminating the path to the rose garden. I lead her there now, to that place where this all began, and where I'll ask her to stay, to be mine, to marry me and lift this curse.

When I first stumbled upon the roses, the scent assailed me so greatly that memories of my humanity leapt forth, and I stumbled. My mind raced as I tried to collect myself, but the perfume of the roses continued to overwhelm. I held my breath and steadied myself, trying to make sense of my surroundings.

Roses were often grown at great personal cost. Not only were the seedlings and upkeep expensive and extensive, they required a certain touch that not everyone possessed. It was hinted that magic was required, though magicians and sorcerers had often tried to breed and grow them at an accelerated pace in hopes of profit, often facing disappointment, if not an outright assault of thorns and briars. Every so often in a family, a patch of previously straggling bushes was left in the care of a new member, and suddenly they would flourish, exploding in riotous color and scent. These few, from all different walks of life, were brought to the royal gardens to train and be trained in the art of botany. Even then, the roses' blooming was intense, often consuming the whole plant in its demise.

These, though, these roses, large as saucers or small as stars, in a million different scents that I was just now beginning to distinguish as I took small sips of air. They were different. If every gardener we'd ever had had devoted their whole lives to nothing but the caring of these roses for seven generations, they might have looked like these. Each was perfection.

"How do you light the lanterns?" she asks.

"I didn't," I say, startled to answer. "Rather, the spirits here did."

"The spirits... the invisible ones?"

"Invisible, intangible, yet they can do more than I can. Life here would be very different without them."

"They can be helpful," she agrees. "I know they're there, behind bends in the air, waiting on me, but whenever I've asked for something specific, they don't do it."

"No, they wouldn't," I muse, recalling my own difficulties with them. "They're here to assist me."

They shocked me when I first met them. After eons in the rose garden, I made my way through the garden's paths and found myself at a castle. I was instinctually weary, having caught man's scent in The Wood, rare, but unmistakable. The castle didn't smell of man, though. It smelt...alive. After careful scouting, I finally stepped inside the open front doors, and they rushed me, a million different little winds, ruffling through my fur and inspecting every inch of me. I froze, immobile. I had no idea how to fight an enemy I couldn't see. But then, I slowly calmed as they made no attack on me, and I could sense them eventually settling, waiting.

After the scents of the rose garden, and this startling discovery, I started to pant. I wondered if there was a stream nearby. I could almost hear them discussing amongst themselves, and then, from the air, a spray of water shot out and hit me in the face.

I jumped, yowling in surprise, and I could hear them take to the air, swirling and zipping as I blinked water out of my eyes. It was hard to understand sound that wasn't sound, but it almost seemed they were laughing.

"So, you can command them?"

I shake my head. "Sometimes they misunderstand my intent, but today, for example, they did everything right."

"Today?"

"Yes. The gowns, the music boxes, the flowers and decorations, the dinner, they understood it all."

A pause, and I sense her mind working, questions brimming. "So, how does it work? How do they get everything?"

"Everything is already here," I answer. She falls silent at that, and I'm unsure what I can add without confusing her too greatly. I've come to accept the castle's unbelievable nature as truth, instinct over logic. Its location remains relatively consistent for The Wood, so I used it as a point of direction in my travels. It became routine to return to it. After all my time alone, even invisible company was welcome. As time passed, I found myself using more of their help in my day-to-day life. In addition to water on demand, I missed the comfort of a fireplace, so I spent a day trying to make them understand the concept of fire. After a few near-disastrous attempts, I got to enjoy a lazy day being warmed by more than sunlight. It was ages before I realized I had come to call the place my home.

We arrive at the garden walls, and I lead her through the hedge into the garden. The crescent moons gleam as bright as their real-life counterpart, and the roses shine warmly in the lantern light. I turned to Rosalind, ready to begin my soliloquy, but she's looking at me in confusion.

"How can you tell them what to do? Did you create them?"

"No, they aren't of this world, but they are held to my biding."

"So, if you ask, and they understand, it happens."

"Sometimes not immediately, but eventually, yes."

She starts to wring her hands. "And they aren't making something out of nothing. Everything is already here."

"I suppose it seems that way." In the wake of Rose's father, I realized I had things to teach I had long forgotten, cooked food and prepared meals being just one aspect. Not that they hadn't tried to feed me in the past, but now I had to convey that the raw meet had to be cooked, bones removed, fruits and breads introduced, for someone who was yet to come. The sparse rooms grew furnishings, at first decidedly beast-shaped, but soon comfortable for the use of man and woman. Wall decorations, statuary and vases, remembrances of my old life.

She looks down at the rings on her fingers, at the dress she's wearing. "The things in my room... who used to own all those beautiful things?"

"No one," I say quickly.

"No one?" she repeats, unconvinced. "The dressing gowns, the combs and scarves, and the dresses. Who was she?"

"Who?"

"The woman whose room that was."

In the days after Rose's father left, only one matter of preparation remained untouched – Rose's room. I had no idea what she would like, what she would need, beyond roses and books, and the castle already had both of those. The spirits, intuitive though they were, needed me to give them an idea of where to start. I had only ever truly known one woman. So I described her likes and dislikes, her clothes, her perfumes and jewelry - all the information I had gathered in our courtship was now used to furnish Rose's room. By the time it was complete, days before her arrival, it was like going back in time. I instructed the spirits to move it, keep its location from me. I had not seen it since.

"It's only your room," I say. I instructed the spirits that Rose was free to change it to match her tastes after her arrival, but I now wonder if she ever did.

"For now," she retorts. She begins pacing, like a cornered animal. I don't understand what is happening. My carefully planned evening is going up in flames, and I'm powerless to stop it. She suddenly halts, looks around her at the flowers.

"This is where it happened, isn't it? Where you... coerced my father into trading his life and the lives of his daughters, and for what? For me to fill the shoes of the woman that was once here?"

"No," I say, trying to infuse my thunderous voice with calm. "Out of loneliness and desperation I struck that deal with your father. I would have never hurt him, surely you must know that."

"I don't know what to think now! I thought you were trapped here, just like me. But you command the invisible, you have enough dresses for a dozen women, and you threatened my family. I should have never forgotten that. And now, after tonight, after all you did for me, I thought..."

"Thought what?"

"I thought you were letting me go." All anger and frustration evaporate out of her, leaving only sadness and the exposed desire of what she really wanted for her birthday, the one thing I can't give her.

"I can't."

"Why not? Please, why not?" Her voice is a strangled whisper. "What do you want of me?"

There's nothing for it. I tell her. "A wife."

She freezes, and I hurry to fill the silence. "I've been here too many years to count, and I had despaired of ever finding solace, until your father came here, and told me of his beautiful daughters. I hoped then, as I hope now, and I wish to ask you to marry me."

Still she does not move, and I see the old terror that had gripped her at the start of our relationship has returned. "Say yes or no, without fear."

Eyes wide and hands clenched, one, two, three heartbeats pass by, then, "No." And she flees, runs down the path like demons are at her heels. I clench, waiting for the main doors to close, and then release a roar of frustration and anger, trying to drown out the despair rising in my chest. I run for the Wood, attempting to escape the inescapable.

Yes.

I woke up with the word in my head, *yes.* No magic pull, just unshakable determination, *yes.* It had been near two months since I last entered the Wood, with days full of cold winds and feverish preparation for the coming winter months. But that day, I dressed quietly, placing the rose around my neck. I left the house in the predawn light, made my way

106

through the frost and reached the river before I even felt the cold. Once across, the sun grew brighter, the air warmer. Every few steps I would see a russet root snaking through the undergrowth, the heartwood, following my path. Unlike before, its heartbeats were quicker, lively. I tried to tread carefully, be logical and cautious, but the beat was infectious. Already I felt lighter, nearly giddy. I felt like running.

Then, there was a quiet footstep behind me. I turned, expecting a dark shadow to emerge, and was amazed to instead see a deer delicately stepping out of the underbrush no more than a stone's throw away. She was small, dappled so exquisitely it was hard to tell where she ended and the shadows began, but her eyes were focused on me. She hadn't bolted, but as the seconds passed, it seemed she had no intention of doing so. Slowly the tension fell from her shoulders, her ears swiveled and she leaned forward to graze. The rumors of the Wood being lifeless grew weaker everyday to me. More likely the hunters, too scared by its strangeness, spread word that there were no animals to hunt there anyway. Perhaps the years without humans had made the animals forget to be wary.

Then she was rigid again, ears and legs akimbo, and I froze myself, wondering if I had scared her. She leapt, tail raised, back into the undergrowth. A second later, a black blur, like a shadow, follows. I knew it was not my imagination that the sounds of the running deer stopped abruptly moments later. The silence stretched, and I was too numb to react when he finally stepped out from behind a nearby tree. There was no blood on his face.

Why today, of all days, did she have to come back? An aching emptiness inside led me to stalk the deer, but even as I broke its neck in my jaws, a different scent filled my head, and I knew she was here, that she had seen. I think for a moment about running, but I am tired. I drop the deer and walk back to her.

"You killed it."

I nod.

"Why?"

I'm unsettled, still reeling from the disappointment of last night. In the dirt, I scratch roughly, *sorry upset you.*

"But not sorry you killed it."

I pause, thrown for a moment, then write, *food.*

"Food," she says quietly. I take a step toward her, and she holds up a hand, a useless gesture, but I stay back. "Of course, food. You need to eat. Of course..."

Still upset.

"No, I'm not...a little, I suppose...I suppose, after all this time, I've remembered you different. That you weren't so...animal."

The word hits me like a tree branch. So, I have finally become what I appear. I write, with great care, *I am an animal.* Easier now, to let her think this of me, what I think of myself.

"But that is just it, you couldn't be. Look at you, you write and think and feel. Animals don't write, animals don't ignore instincts." She kneels down, tries to look me in the eye. "You aren't an animal."

The closer she gets to the truth, the more I need to push her away. I can feel her unspoken questions, the questions about my existence, who I am and how I came to be what I am, the questions I both desire and fear to answer. From the well of despair inside me comes a roar, loud as thunder that I release in agony, exposing my sharpened fangs and monstrous gullet, screaming wordlessly *this is what I am now.* When it ends, I expect to see terror in her face, but her face is calm, her eyes still locked on mine. With no word, she opens her arms, leans forward, and wraps herself around my neck.

Beyond hope and trust, with death roaring in my face, I instinctively leaned in and gripped his dark fur. I felt his throat contract as he released another cry, this one quieter, but ragged. It sounded like a heart breaking, but I didn't know if it was his or my own now shattered. He hung his heavy head over my shoulder in a not quite animal, not quite human gesture, and I twined my fingers softly in his fur, wanting to comfort him with words, but unable to find any suitable. I instead focused on this moment between us. This silent interaction, the first time I had ever touched him, was more important than exchanging stilted words. I slowly moved my hands over his shoulders, feeling the skin and muscles beneath the thick fur. With my forehead buried between his throat and shoulder, I inhaled the scent of him, fluid and clear and alive. Afraid of restraining him long, I loosened my grip to fall back, but his chin stiffened and held me there. Within the depths of him, a rhythmic beat reverberated – purring, or what you could call purring in an animal bigger than a horse. I grinned and went back to stroking his fur, content to stay with him for a moment longer.

Too soon I let her go, too soon she is gone across the river. After she disappears, I make my way back to the fallen doe. She is arched on the ground, legs outstretched as if she is still running. I've nearly forgotten the existence of a higher power, and this deer is just a deer, but even so, I bow down before it, a virgin offering to unquenchable hunger. When I lift my head, I'm startled to find the doe completely covered in a mound of pale slender vines, twisted and twirled around each other and speckled with glowing white flowers. I can no longer make out her shape or her scent. It is easy to believe that there is no longer a deer here, that flesh has turned to ferns and she has returned to what she was made from. I leave the magical bower and head back to the castle.

NINE

ENCHANTMENTS

I don't see Rosalind all day, and I don't try to find her. I'm sure she has no desire to listen to anything I have to say. To be honest, I'm not sure I have anything else to say. All of my weeks of work were for nothing. I am still the monstrous captor. The game hasn't changed, it's just gone back to how it always was, and I've laid out what I need of her. I am beyond surprised when she does arrive at dinner that night, but I do not question it. It is all I have left. Dinner is silent once more, except when she stands to leave.

"Rosalind."

She stops, one hand clenched on the tablecloth. "Yes?"

"Will you marry me?"

She turns to meet my gaze, for the first time that evening. "No, Beast." I hear the anger, the fear, the sadness, the pain all rolled up in those two words as she leaves. I don't go running for the door, nor do I sit and brood. I wait a few moments, then also leave and head for my room. No dreams for me tonight, no restless worries or regret. What is done, is done, and I have no fear of waiting. I've grown accustomed to waiting silently in the dark these many years, and I fall asleep quickly.

In the morning, I return to the river. When she finally arrives across the river, I am not surprised.

"How long have you been here?" she asks as she lands on my side of the river.

Long enough.

She smiles, a light in the shadows. "May we walk a little together? Unless you'd like to make another startling entrance later on today."

Maybe tomorrow.

She laughs this time. "After you, then."

We walked in silence for some time, side by side when the space between trees allowed it, which allowed me to get better looks at him. I was fascinated with how his limbs moved. With one step, definitely wolf, but then another, and it was a lion. Then the shoulders would shift, and it would be the shudder in a horse's flanks, the tail twitch of a fox as it ran. Then I would catch his eyes looking towards me, and quickly look ahead to avoid some low-hanging branch that never once appeared.

I feel her gaze on me, but I don't begrudge her these looks. I find my eyes lingering on her too. I am intrigued, but unlike the unreadable mystery of silent, still Rosalind, I am able to understand her body as it moves through the Wood. She is confident, sure of her steps. When she isn't looking at me, her eyes remain alert, scanning her surroundings instead of downcast at her feet. Curious, then. Perhaps too curious – she does continue to come back when common sense should keep her away. But then, I am failing in much the same way.

Even before the heartwood had reached thickness greater than myself, I somehow felt I knew where we were going, and was not surprised to see the giant tree come into view, still too big to be believed. I took the lead now, carefully navigating the nearest root. After a few moments, I turned back, but he had disappeared. Momentarily confused, a few falling leaves alerted me to his presence above in the branches. I continued walking, keeping an eye out till I found a branch snaking by. Before I could truly contemplate what I was about to attempt, I quickly leapt to it, and I was off the ground. It was perhaps luck that the branch I had chosen was actually three branches, snaking around each other to form gaps and ridges that served as ideal placements for hands and feet. That, and my months of manual labor, helped me to climb the slowly inclining branch, though I became increasingly aware of the wind tousling my hair and dress. I could sense him nearby, watching my progress. Before my limbs grew too taxed, the branch leveled off, and I half crawled onto relatively solid ground. Refusing to determine how high off the ground I had climbed, I instead looked ahead to see how far away the trunk was. But I was confused by a myriad of trees in my way. I suddenly realized the softness of the ground beneath my feet, and looked down to see dirt, grass, flowers, and the roots of a host of trees, some no bigger than saplings, some as tall as those on the ground below. Beyond all conceivability, the intertwined branches had collected enough soil, water and sunlight to sustain a miniature forest.

"Trees in the tree," I said to myself. "I really shouldn't be so surprised anymore by these little departures from reality."

A growling chuckle told me he'd joined me on the floating forest. "Look who I'm talking to," I said as I turned to face him. He was standing in the shade of a cedar tree, darker than the shadows that hid him. I walked over to him. "I seem to continually find myself out of my depths whenever I cross the river. Is the entire Wood like this?"

He sat and scrawled the word, *Often,* in the dirt before him. I sat down beside him with my back in the dappled sunlight so it could warm me.

"Do you know why?"

Hard to say.

"Or spell."

Another chuckle. *Wood always wild, but sometimes hidden.*

"You make it sound like an..." I trailed off, suddenly unsure of my words. He wasn't, though.

Animal.

"Yes," I said, a little embarrassed. "But then, it just is what it is. It's my perception of it that makes it scary or unbelievable. A tree can't be anything but itself."

Are you sure?

His comment gave me pause.

I busy myself with wiping away all the words I have written, willing her to forget what I've just asked, and wondering what her silence means. When my words have vanished, I write out, *Tree more than tree.*

"I suppose so," she says slowly, emerging from her own thoughts. "You mean this one, don't you? It's a tree, but it's a world onto itself, and I imagine its roots run through the entire Wood."

I nod.

"It is truly alive, isn't it?" She leans back to look up at the canopy overhead, and the sunlight plays across her face, white and black, day and night. After never-ending days and eternal nights, the interaction of the two on her face is almost dizzying. I am falling, and I want to keep falling, and I cannot.

I look back to see him staring at me, but I cannot read his expression. "Is this what makes the Wood wild, what...brought you here?"

The silence stretches. Finally, he writes, *What brought you here?*

"Good question," I reply, momentarily stymied. I somehow knew the half-hearted lies I had been telling myself about why I continued to return to the Wood wouldn't pass muster under his gaze, the way you couldn't trick a horse into thinking you were a seasoned rider when you weren't. When else would I be free to be this honest, this open, with myself? "I suppose...when I first came, I was trying to escape. I was looking for something more than myself. If there was more to my world than I knew, then maybe there was a place where I could be..." I trailed off, knowing what I felt, but unable to phrase it. I lightly shrugged. "Not the most elegant of phrasing, but I've never been a wordsmith."

A place where you could be more.

He knew. The careful etching in the dirt told me he knew it even more than I did. "That's it, yes. More." I looked out over the edge of the branch, across the canopy of trees. "Is there more, that you could show me?"

Yes. Much more.

"Very good," I said. "I want to see more. That is, as soon as I figure out how to get down off this tree."

From that day on, there wasn't a week that went by that we didn't meet. From the banks of the river, he took me into the depths of the Wood, where reality-defying sights appeared so often I would have thought they'd become commonplace to me, but every time, I found them amazing. We found a misty glen which went down into the earth beyond sight, a waterfall that sent its water upwards into the heavens, a tree laden with every fruit under the sun that would promptly put you to sleep for an indefinite age should you so foolishly pick and eat one, or so he told me to keep me from trying one myself. I wanted to challenge him on that, but after seeing three robins asleep in the grass around a fallen apple, I didn't question him further.

Some days, we got no father than the heartwood tree. My initial climbs, based on no more than intuition and strong grips, grew more ambitious as my skills improved, though I knew I would never climb as high as he could, and climbing down still left me unnerved, no matter how many times I'd accomplished it before. As I climbed, I discovered different branches yielded different flora, depending on the height and amount of sunlight the branch received. One particularly shaded branch was little more than a carpet of the little star-white flowers, which we laid in and looked up at the interweaving of the canopy so tight-knit it resembled the night sky itself, where gaps in the leaves shone bright as the flowers beneath us.

Even on days when we didn't encounter anything more remarkable than flowers in a clearing, the stretching of time was intriguing within itself. I learned that the sun would move less the farther into the Wood we went, and eventually appear to stop, no matter how long we walked. Over the weeks, I saw the sun, which had always been high in the time

I'd been here, start to circle lower to the horizon. He couldn't explain it perfectly in our strange exchanges, but it made sense if I didn't think too much about it. At home, I no longer made excuses to leave, or even tried very hard to hide it, but Giselle didn't comment, and I looked forward to leaving the deepening winter for eternally sunny afternoons. I was happy when exploring the Wood. More so, I was happy to explore it with him. Even in his silence, he was a great comfort. When we did talk, I found him to be honest and surprisingly funny. It was so easy to admit that I was drawn to the excitement, the adventure of it all, and with him, I saw so much.

He would always lead us back to the river by sunset, seeming to know the passage of time without the movement of the sun, and after a few journeys, I began to learn how he guided us, the russet roots growing ever smaller until disappearing at the river's edge. At first unsure of what it would mean to him, it was soon too easy for me to stroke his head before crossing the river, and he never objected.

One day, the river had swelled from snowfall, and I remembered that cold starry night that we had first encountered each other as I stared at the roaring water. He waited, motionless but not impassive at my careful crossing, and as I slid onto solid ground, I saw his shoulders relax, his fur lay flat on his spine. "I wish it didn't bother me still," I said as I untied my skirt and draped my winter cloak over a tree branch. "I am unfamiliar with water. The most I ever saw was the lake on our summer trips when I was a child, but we only ever went sailing once, and I couldn't even see the water from the deck of the clipper. Not much chance to swim in the city, even less in the country."

I turned to him, and a light had entered his eyes, the tips of his canines gleaming under his curling lips. "What?" I accused. "You think I'm afraid?" He didn't respond, but took off through the trees, and after a half moment of hesitation, I ran after him. When I eventually caught up to him, he was still smiling and walked through a curtain of hanging branches. I parted them and enter a shady glen. In its center lay a pool, gem-like in its crystal stillness. As I got closer, I saw the turquoise shallows fade into dark and deepening green, the floor covered in rounded stones. I'd seen enough magic here to hesitate to touch the water, but he walked in before me, and did not change. He turned back to me, ripples echoing across the pool's surface, waiting. I raised an eyebrow.

"I think we've established before that I cannot swim."

One dripping paw came back to the dry ground at my feet. *Teach you.*

"That's alright, I don't need to know."

Want to know?

That gave me pause. I assessed his gaze, but there was only hope in his eyes. I leaned down, slipped off my boots and eyed my skirt. I remembered it heavy and constricting in the freezing river. A small breath, and then I slipped out of it, standing in only my bodice and linen drawers. His expression did not change. As I stepped into the water, I was pleased to discover it pleasantly cool after the run through the Wood. I followed him as he treaded backwards through the pool, and the water was soon past my knees. I unclenched my hands and let them trail behind me, spread and float as I sank down to my waist. He began to paddle his front paws, and I copied his movements as the water lapped at my shoulders, feet still on the pebbled ground. The movement propelled me forward, and, emboldened, I kicked my feet behind me. I must have looked a flailing fool, but he focused on my movements, showing better ways to turn my hands and feet to cut through the water. I circled the shallows repeatedly, my limbs slowly learning how to move, and I branched out wider, sometimes sinking down and pushing off the ground with my feet for extra speed. Then came the time when my foot reached down into emptiness, and I realized I'd gone too far before I slipped down under the water.

And then I was out of the water, as something pushed me up. He had already swum up beneath me, and now we both were cutting through the water like a cantering horse. He let me catch my breath, and then cut back down through the water. I dared to open my eyes, and discovered a dazzling melted world of liquid light playing off my arm, his fur, the greenery swaying at the bottom of the pool and, of course, the heartwood roots, just as beautifully russet underwater as above. We burst up again, and I laughed, sliding off his back, but leaving one arm around his neck as we swam back to shore.

I collapsed on dry land, tired and exhilarated all at once. He shook himself vigorously like a dog, water cascading off him as the trees shifted in the breeze, and sun sharply entered the glen. Every inch of him was illuminated, radiant and on fire. The blackness of him expanded, filling my vision till I felt blinded. And then I blinked, and he receded, still big, but not earth-shatteringly big, with fur sticking out in thick spikes. I laughed, and ran my fingers through my hair, feeling my own tangled mess. He walked over and sat by me as I combed out my twisted hair. Then I turned my hands to him and worked out his snarls as he lay back, growling soft enough to be mistaken for a purr.

We finally sit in the eternally setting sun together, her body resting in the curve of mine. The warmth of her is dizzying. Drowsy to the point of comatose, I can't remember a time when I was more content. I can hear the clouds racing in the sky beyond the trees, but on the ground the wind barely stirs my fur. "Do you ever wish you could fly?" she asks. A snort escapes me. I have wished for many things in my exile, but flying has never been one of them. "Well, I do, sometimes," she replies defiantly. I open one eye to look at her as she gazes towards the sky. "What it must be like, to see the curve of the world below you, to go anywhere? Like falling and never landing, always your stomach in your throat and excitement in your mouth." She turns her head down towards me. "Or like swimming, I suppose, if I ever get any good."

Takes a while.

"How long did it take you?"

Few weeks. Kept opening my mouth.

She laughs, and I feel it reverberate through my own body. I draw closer around her, intoxicated by her warmth, her scent. She closes her eyes, smiling. "Well, I'll remember that for next time."

Next time. There will be a next time. How long can it last, though? This friendship, if you can call it that, is the truest thing I have in my life, and it is still a lie. At least with Rosalind she knows where I stand, even if I tell her little else. For months I have tried to plan and create, to understand our relationship, and still I know the only thing keeping her here is fear for her father's safety. It is this slim thread I tread that keeps my hope alive, and that I know will soon break. Surely she cannot still fear me. But maybe I am confusing the only two women in my life.

I feel her sigh, then lean up and reach over for her skirt. I remain motionless while she redresses. Even I do not want to over think my reactions to this, both man and animal disconcertingly in sync. "And to think, beyond the trees, winter has fallen," she says, tying up her ribbons. "I forget, sometimes, that there is a place where it isn't always summer." We walk back to the river in amiable silence. She grabs her cloak off the branch. "Do you like it here?"

Mostly. Miss snow. If it covered everything around me, I could more easily forget how all the color has disappeared from my world.

She looks across the bank at the soft white shore and nods. "Snow is beautiful, though decidedly less so when it's leaking through your roof, or clogging up your chimney."

I chuckle, and she looks back at me. "Why don't you come over with me? We can enjoy the snow for a moment."

Cannot.

She is quiet, but her eyes scream questions, questions I want to answer, but must rebuff. *You live there, I live here.* My breath hangs in my chest, hoping for her to accept this flimsy reason. She nods, and I exhale in relief as she runs a hand along my brow, before making her way back across the river. She adjusts her clothes on the far bank, stark against the snow, and I turn to leave, a note of sadness threatening the wonderful memories of today. Then, suddenly, a blast of ice and cold hits the side of my face, and I shake the snow free from my eyes quick enough to see her laughing and running up the hill, disappearing into the snowy Wood.

Winter was upon us, the cozy hamlet we lived in now constantly dusted in snowfall. The edges of the lakes and rivers began to freeze, and it became hard to tell where the chimney smoke ended and the grey sky began. We had invested in new rugs, furs and candles. We tried to be basic, but with never-ending wealth, we sometimes chose the softer sable over the stiffer brown, the scented candles, the patterned rugs. Perhaps our hamlet wasn't so small, as none questioned where we were getting our extra coin. Or, perhaps more surprisingly, these people were kinder. We never suffered scrutiny here like we did in the city, where every move was measured, every gesture was meant to be seen. We never felt like we had no privacy, but rather our lives were set upon a stage, part of a larger play. Here, we were the background characters, the stagehands, going about our business for the audience's gaze to pass over without a second glance. The story of how we came here may have been unique, but our novelty had long passed. We were now one of them.

Our larger income, and my winter preparations, appeared to have done us well, which left me more and more free time that I was loathe to spend indoors when there was a sunny day waiting beyond the river. My thoughts began to drift like snowflakes, landing on questions that had been easier to ignore in the summer heat.

I wanted to know about spells, castings and sorcery. There were no libraries in Magnasaltus, so I charted a path over the frosty hills to visit the home of the garden witch.

Gossip in town gave me good directions to where she dwelt, but when I arrived at the low door set in a hillock of earth, I was momentarily unnerved. The only prior experience I had with magicians was the Count of Viscarrie's tower, and this hole in the ground was nothing like that. Had I been less determined, I might have turned and left when a severe faced woman, cloaked and stooped, answered the door. But there were things I had to know.

"Good morrow," I said quickly. "My name is Evelyn Cavanaugh, I hope I'm not interrupting you, but if you have a moment, I was hoping you could-"

"Curse, charm or ward?" she listed without batting an eye. Clearly, others had visited her before, searching for magical answers to their own questions.

"All," I said, and her eyes suddenly focused on mine, narrowed and piercing. I rushed to clarify. "I'm not exactly sure what I'm looking for, I'm sorry, I've never really spoken to a garden witch, I only have limited experience with magic casters, make that one sorcerer, many years ago, that's not really important to this conversation, but I suppose I'd be interested in information, on magic, in general. Please."

She held my eyes a moment more, then swiftly turned. "Come in," she said as she disappeared back inside. I followed her and nearly tripped on a short set of stairs leading into the earth. I stumbled to the floor and was amazed to realize I could stand straight, with the ceiling arching high above my head into a dome. I was only a little surprised to see heartwood roots growing above our heads across the room, laden with warmly glowing lanterns. Jars and vials, neatly labeled and stacked, stood in niches carved into the earthen walls. The floor beneath me was covered in grass mats, woven into complex patterns and designs that flowed like water. I tore my gaze from my surroundings to see the garden witch standing by a simmering cauldron. The grey smoke rising from it turned blue as she added liquid from an urn she held to the concoction. She reached up to hang the urn on a root above her, and I realized she was taller than I. She slid her cloak off, revealing loose slacks strapped at the ankles, and a practical tunic bound across her midsection with a complex wrapping and overlapping technique, not unlike the woven mats.

"Garden witches, they call us," she said as she removed a pair of enormous bellows from a hook on the wall and began to stoke the embers under the cauldron. "Paints an idyllic enough scene, little old ladies making tinctures out of pansies, curing warts and strengthening plows. Certainly, we are connected to the earth, why we surround ourselves with it, live in it. But magic is more than the physical limitations of matter." The embers flared to life, and she removed the bellows and took two jars off an earthen shelf. "There is only so much the earth can provide," she said as she measured powder in her hands before adding it to the brew.

I wondered if she was even still talking to me. "What name do you prefer, then?"

"I have always been partial to magic weavers, much more descriptive of what I do, but you can just call me Ilena."

"Ilena," I said. "Pleasure to meet you."

"Properly, at least," she said, and I must have look confused. "I see you often at the edges of the Wood. You are there more often than I." She pauses, perhaps waiting for explanations, but I don't offer any. "Well, Evelyn Cavanaugh, if you are looking for knowledge on magic, I can tell you what I know, but even with your limited interactions with sorcerers, you must know that we do not give something for nothing."

"What would you want?"

"You could give me the shine from your hair, or the color of your eyes." She let those possibilities hang in the air, but then gave a chuckle as the fire dwindled again. "But for now, I could use more firewood."

Over the next few weeks, I chopped bundle after bundle of firewood, shoveled a path through the snow from her door to the road, brought food from town, and did many other mundane chores for Ilena. In exchange, she taught me about various types of magic, not in any coherent manner that I could tell, but random knowledge dropped in the midst of my tasks, not that I could have offered direction in any way, having no idea where to start myself. It was a week before she presented my first possible option, familiars. Animals that served a magical master seemed likely at first, but I eventually learned that they were actually physical manifestations of spiritual beings and took the shape of animals that already existed in our world, not like the unnamable creature I spent my afternoons with.

Another day, while I chopped, peeled, and ground up dried herbs, she spoke about experimentation, animals created from other animals, but taught to think, write, and reason. This practice, she told me in somber tones, died several hundred years ago, too dangerous and with disastrous, often deadly, consequences.

Weeks passed, and there seemed less and less work for me to do for Ilena, but her knowledge did not run out, and she did not request more of me. Some days, we sat by her hearth and I listened, entranced, as she led me through the various magical elements she had worked with or encountered.

"Why did you choose to settle here?" I asked Ilena one day as she sat at a low table, pulling apart skeins of wool I had bought for her in town. "You know as much as any sorcerer, you would have been honored in a city."

She gave me a wry smile that let me know she thought me naively foolish, a common occurrence in our talks. "Yes, as you can see, I clearly yearn for the exquisite comforts of wealth," she said, sweeping one hand around her humble dwelling. "It was not a choice, not one that I made consciously. I was inquisitive and curious on the ways of magic, and after years of studying, I was led here, and I turned this hill into my home. I learned much from the teachings of others, but you require more than knowledge to become one as I, such as a special connection with the network of the ether."

"Ether?"

"The beyond. The web of magic and power that wrap around the world." She extended her fingers, strands looping between her hands. "Where they intersect, great magic resides." She pulled the strings taught. "The sorcerers in cities, they pull the web to fit around their homes. The harder they pull, the tighter the tangles and the more volatile it becomes. Thus, their reputations grow, even as they expend more and more power to bend it to their will." She slid her fingers out of the looped skein, set it on two slender rods, and began to wind. "But those like me, those who feel the ether, they are drawn to the strong points, the wilds and the wastes, and settle there, adding to the web."

"Do you not get lonely?"

"It depends on what makes you feel alone," she said simply. "I would feel more alone in a city surrounded by hundreds, then here, connected to the ether. With the Wood so close, even a single strand is multiplied ten fold in strength."

"What makes it so powerful?" I asked curiously.

She didn't answer at first, instead tying off the bundle and placing it in the basket by her side. As she pulled another skein apart, she said quietly, almost musing to herself, "We have no idea whether the intertwining of magic created the

Wood, or the Wood gathered the magic around itself. But," she said more alertly, "with that much magic at play, we naturally gravitate towards it. We can only work within it for so long, of course. Too long, and we'd lose ourselves in it."

"Like some travelers," I said, thinking of my own father.

"It is more than the loss of a body, it is the loss of our mind. Those affected by or in tune with magic can lose parts of themselves. That is why I never enter the Wood. I keep to the boundaries, as close as I can get, without losing myself."

"Can spells be worked within it?"

"If so, it has never been documented," she said, winding the newest looped skein. "Most spells worked there dissipate into pure energy and are absorbed by the Wood itself. But whatever magic I bring in from outside it stays firm, perhaps even stronger."

I now wondered whether the creeping of time was something the Wood had always possessed, or had been cast upon it by his enchantment. Neither sounded particularly simple, but I was hopeful that its difficulty meant it was unlikely a sorcerer cast it, more likely the nature of the Wood itself, and his enchantment, therefore, more manageable.

"Of course, you would know more about the nature of the Wood than I would," Ilena said, and I turned sharply to see her still winding, eyes focused on her task. "You are welcome to your secrets, and I would not assume to know what you are looking for in there, but the crossing of that much magic is dangerous. You think you are following one strand, but eventually it will lead into another, and then you will be tangled in it too."

That week, she spoke on enchantments. Unlike the other magical arts, enchantments created a binding network of rules and restrictions that trapped the victim within the spell, with only one way out. The strongest of these, curses, seemed like passion plays to an outside viewer, but I learned they were the most calculated and difficult of enchantments to enact, requiring great care, and the cure coming about only through great change and sacrifice. The more I thought on it as I walked back home and floated through my own chores, the more this seemed the most likely option. These rules could account for his inability to cross the river, even though he could swim, or his reticence to discuss himself or his past. However, it was impossible to tell how he came to be this way, or what he was before, without knowing the parameters of the spell. He may not even have been the target of this enchantment, but just caught in the crossfire of higher powers.

It seemed I had an answer to my question, a place to start my plans and schemes, but they remained half-formed without a direction to head in. The snowfall grew heavier as winter deepened, and often we were confined to our house. Some days, we were unable to even open the door without letting drifts up to our waists fall inside. I threw myself into my housework, always moving so I wouldn't notice how cramped and close our living quarters now seemed. The harsh grey light reflecting off the snow through the windows made everything sharper, from headaches to tongues.

When I awoke one chilly winter morning from a dream of shadows with teeth and strange eyes, I suddenly knew. Foolish, how could I not have seen it before? Maybe I didn't want to see it, but it had been in front of me for months. The monster that had demanded my sister's life clearly had power beyond human ken. My friend must know where his castle was, if only to avoid it. I had never told him about my family, or what had happened to Rose. Who would know better than he where my sister is? But it could be even more. What if the monster that had my sister was responsible for the enchantment on my friend?

It didn't feel right to ask, and what if he could not say? The enchantment upon him could lay too thick for him to provide any answers, as it already seemed to keep him silent about his past. On days I had managed to carve out enough snow to make it to the Wood, I had tried to encourage him to talk on his circumstances, but he remained silent or changed the subject, never purposefully, it seemed, but increasingly conveniently. I thought again and again about opening up and revealing my quest, and asking any knowledge of his and my sister's captor, but I remained silent.

The eternal days in the Wood were gone, and the darkness beyond the sunset grew. I finally felt ready, and when I departed from him one day, I stood behind a tree beyond the ridge, and peered around to watch him walk away. Then I knelt in the snow and uncovered a small knapsack with food and water, a knife and rope, and a small lantern with tinder that I had left there that morning. I quickly went back across the river and entered the Wood where he had, silently tracking the quivering branches and heartwood roots in the gathering dark. Ilena's warnings on the tangling of the ether reverberated in my mind, and I strained my eyes, as if I would see the web around me.

The darkness, while not as dark as it should be for all the trees eclipsing the starry sky above, was still deep, and I had a fleeting thought that I should turn back, go home and sleep, but there was an urge inside me to know what was happening, even if I didn't understand it, as much as there was an urge to go back to the Wood after falling in the river. If I hadn't, I wouldn't have met my friend. Maybe I'd find some answers. The silence of the Wood was echoing, and I pulled out my small blade. It was unlikely to do any damage to whatever may mean me harm, but was rather a symbol of my quickly fading bravery. It at least gave me something to hold in the night, and the glint of the silver was like a star I could follow.

I wonder at her quiet distance as I slink through the Wood. We have walked in silence before, but today, it feels like she trapped her words in her mouth, afraid to let them out. I could hear it in the erratic beat of her heart. She feels so far away. I had stayed with her longer than normal, hoping to wait it out, but she barely looked back when she left. Rosalind had surely eaten dinner by now, gone to bed relieved, no doubt, that she had missed my offer of marriage for a night. Discontent and anger begin to roll around in my skull, down my spine and into my haunches as I prowl through the undergrowth. The gathering darkness puts me on edge. I need to hunt.

As clear as a bell, I suddenly know I am being followed. I let the animal side take over, all instinct and senses, and turn back.

I leaned against a tree, breathing a little heavier than normal after walking for what felt like hours in the dark. I thought I had been making good progress, but I was beginning to wonder if I should risk the lantern, as the heartwood roots had all but disappeared in the darkness. I could just stop for the night. I could just call out for him. But now shame had crept into my thoughts at my sneaking and deception, and just a hint too much pride to admit defeat. I let the knapsack fall to the ground, and then I heard something else hit the ground nearby. I froze, hairs quivering on the back of my neck as I strained my eyes at the gloom around me.

Quick breathing.
Quicker heartbeat.
Blood moving. Tense. Wait. Wait.
Lunge.

The darkness to my right moved too fast, and I lashed out with the blade. A small shriek escaped my lungs. And then, I suddenly realized what I've done. I fumbled for the tinder and strike at the wick in the lantern. The sudden flame illuminated the bloody blade in my hand, and there he stood, staring over his shoulder at me.

My mind returns, and I'm in shock at the dark blood running down her arm. Then, I realize it's mine.

"Oh gods..."
He stared at my hand, and I dropped the blade, hands shaking as I reached towards him, and then held back.
"Oh gods. I am...so sorry. I should have said...oh, your face."
His shoulders shook, rippled and his eyes blinked and focused on mine. He turned to sit down, his bloody face in profile, and he seemed to shrink in the light of the fire, from shadowy immensity to mere physical enormity. I knelt down beside him, as close as I dared.
"You're hurt." He didn't try to deny it, as if the blood running from the gash in his cheek wasn't enough to confirm it. I hesitated a moment longer, then reached for the knapsack again and pulled out the water flask. I inched closer to him and dampened the hem of my winter cloak, and swiftly pressed it to the gash. His canines show as he pulled his lips back in a grimace, but he didn't pull away.
"I am so sorry," I said quietly as I began to dab. "This is all my fault. I shouldn't have followed you. It was wrong, and I...I don't know what I was thinking." I pulled back the fabric to see the blood clotting. It was a clean cut, and should heal nicely. I poured some of the water on his face and applied a new section of cloak. The scar may fade, but I would always know it was there. "Please forgive me."

I can't feel the wound, but I can feel the blood and water running down my face. I can feel her hand, the warmth of it through the cloth. Most of all, I feel deeply troubled. I could have hurt her so easily. I'm more surprised that I didn't. Did the human in me fight its way through to alter my leap, or did my animal side sense enough to realize that it was friend, not foe?
I realize she has asked me a question, and now silently dabs at my face, face drawn and eyes damp. I push the dark troubles away and

turn into her hand to look in her eyes. Her tears threaten to spill over, but she offers a small smile. Her hand rests on my cheek, and I nudge it away to see my dark blood coating it, gathering in the creases of her palm. I instinctively start to clean it. She sits still while I lick her knuckles, run my tongue along her slender fingers. Her hands look rougher than they feel. I get into the same rhythm I have while grooming, moving along the delicate underside of her wrist. I look up after a while, and she is staring at me with a look I have never seen before, on her or any other. I continue until her hand is clean, then use my paw and tongue to clean my cheek. She pours water on it after every few strokes, which isn't necessary, but helpful, and soon we are both clean from my blood.

I move my paw into the light. *Home?*

She nods, but the nod nearly transitions into sleep. I laugh low. *Ride.*

Her eyes question me, so I lie down beside her, my back at her waist, and look back. She packs up the tinder and rolls up the cloak, and finally blows out the lantern. In the dark, she puts a hand on my shoulder blade, then pressure as she swings a knee over and straddles me. I stand up, easily supporting her weight, and start to walk through the trees.

In the darkness, it was easy to rest my head on the base of his neck and let the rhythmic movement of his legs lull me deeper into sleep. I couldn't even feel the ground beneath me, just fur and blackness. "Even my old pony couldn't step as smoothly as you. And you're much bigger than my pony," I muttered. I felt the low rumble of laughter in his chest, and I smiled even as my eyelids drooped. "I don't think you'll need a saddle or bit, though, unless you become unreasonable."

This time I heard the laughter, and it brought a little light to the darkness in my mind. "I am sorry," I said again, knowing it wouldn't be the last time I say it. "I should have just asked to come with you. But you would have said no, I'm sure, for reasons you can't or won't reveal." I stifled a yawn, and I caught the glint of his eye as he turned his head back towards me. "If you can have secrets, then I can have secrets too," and I stifled another yawn. He grunted and turned back forward, and I clasped my arms around his neck, resting my cheek between his shoulder blades as sleep took me.

Her weight is as comforting as her constant deep breaths. Her hands remain clasped at my chest, even in sleep. These moments are so easy, unplanned and perfect, unlike anything else in my life. In other lives, in other times, maybe they could be more than just moments.

Again, I wonder, if I had done nothing when the man came to my castle, if I had let him go and not made him trade his life for his daughter's, then would everything be different now? Could this woman and I have become more than friends?

I laugh even as I lie to myself. We are more than friends, at least in my mind. The tenuous relationship between Rosalind and myself is frustrating, difficult, and inconsistent, but I've been taken by easy love before. Maybe a relationship is supposed to be hard, with work making the bond stronger. Freedom from my curse is close, closer than it has ever been, but Rosalind...she does not love me. It does not hurt as much as I thought it would to admit that. I am fond of her, and care for her, but my heart...maybe I no longer have a human heart, capable of love.

Maybe I'm just telling myself that to make sure I don't get hurt again.

- TEN -
COMPLICATIONS

After returning to the castle and dreaming in a fitful sleep all day, I go to the dining hall, but am surprised to see Rosalind standing outside, leaning against a column, reading a book. As I draw near, she looks up and snaps the book shut, face calm. Her hair looks more carefully placed than last night, than most of the nights we've spent together. Her dress is one of the nicer ones, and she wears a ribbon choker with small stones that gleam like a line of tears. I pause, but before I can think of something to say, she smiles, opens the door and ushers me in. Her demeanor does not change as she goes to her seat, and waits for me to stand at my place before beginning to fill her plate. She starts to talk about what she did that day, observations she made in the book she is reading, the birds she managed to coax down from the sky with the remains of her breakfast. It is pleasant, easy conversation, like it was before her birthday celebration. I am utterly amazed and confused. As she cuts a piece of berry cordial cake for desert, I have to know.

"Rosalind, I'm sure this will be a foolish question, and I should keep quiet, but why are you acting this way?"

She pauses in cutting the cake, but her face remains smooth and she quickly resumes serving herself a piece. "You did not come to dinner last night."

That is not the answer I was expecting.

She continues, "I believe I need to apologize."

That is even more unexpected. "You have nothing to apologize for," I automatically assure her. "Your actions were understandable."

She shakes away my routine assurances with a hand. "I know that ever since… I have been distant. But last night, I came down to dinner, and you never came. At first, I admit, I was relieved. But then, I wondered where you were. You've never missed dinner. You don't eat a thing, but you still always come. I waited for you, so long that the dishes started clearing themselves."

She looks at me. "I worried about you."

"You…." I trail off, more and more confused. "But why?"

It is her turn to look confused. "I don't like hurting you every night, you must know that, and I know that it isn't easy for you to ask either. Regardless of that, we are still two creatures thrown together and we must learn to live with that."

"That may be a little difficult to achieve."

"Maybe so, but it would be better than the silence."

That I agree with. The past few weeks have been so quiet, I could hear the stones breathing. My afternoons in the Wood help me forget, but I still have to return every night to a hushed dinner, and a woman who does not trust me anymore than I trust her. The only words spoken between us have been my entreaty for her hand in marriage, and her inevitable rejection.

"You understand," I say carefully, "that I cannot change what I ask."

"Yes," she says, the fingers of one hand bunching and smoothing her napkin on the table. "I understand. But, until that moment every night, we can be...friends?" Her voice wavers her statement into a question.

"Friends," I repeat. She waits, bunching, smoothing. "We can try."

Her hand releases the napkin. "Very well. We'll try." She stands and squares her shoulders. "Ask me."

"Will you marry me?"

"No."

"Goodnight Rosalind."

"Goodnight Beast."

Rosalind starts to meet with me in the day, catching me returning from hunts and walking the grounds with me for a few hours. She seems to have figured out that I prefer earth under my feet and trees above me. We stick to the lit gardens around the castle, a haven of light within the hours of night, and a safe topic to fall back on if conversation dies. She starts carrying a naturalist book for reference when she comes across a flower neither of us can name. She becomes remarkably quick at recognizing flora, though I have some knowledge to offer in turn, when I save her from touching some deadly hemlock, masquerading as queen's lace, by smelling the poison. This leads to conversations about my heightened animal senses, but it isn't until we get to the rose garden and she attempts to show me the difference in two flowers that look identical to my eyes, that she learns I am colorblind. I assure her that it doesn't hinder me, and at night, it is hardly noticeable, but she gives me a pitying look I've been seeing more and more from her. She likes to keep coming back to the rose garden, and though I was hesitant when we first entered, she showed no sign of its significance, only joy at its loveliness. I am glad she finds happiness in it, but I often leave her there, unable to remain too long in the memory of what has happened here, what has brought us both to this place.

The roses had brought her to me, just as I had been told. When I had been cursed, after I had come to grips with my fur and fangs, the animal ache for the hunt and the disappearance of color, I forced myself to remember every detail she had told me, knowing they were the clues to my eventual release. The one detail I kept coming back to was the rose garden. *The roses would bring us together.* I had awoken in a rose garden. There were days I did not move from the center of that garden, waiting as she had said, even when the scent of the flowers nearly drove me to madness. *Wait for true love.* After endless months I gave up on its powers, until the man came. The man with daughters, caught in my debt with stolen roses in his hands, had given me hope that I would soon be free. Then Rosalind had come, and now I couldn't stand the roses, the reminders. Every tenuous thread that connects us seems tainted by the past, and I do not see a way to fix that.

Ironically, my growing hesitance is met with Rosalind's growing enthusiasm. She is always around me now, filling my usually silent days with chatter and smiles, and though pleasant, it is strange. What was revealed to her the night that I didn't come back for dinner that has changed her demeanor so radically? Could she really find me good company? Could we really be friends? Or is she merely no longer afraid?

Our walks grow longer, and my journeys into the Wood grow more and more infrequent. When I see the girl from the river, she makes no mention of missing me, or how many days it has been since we last met. I come to find that she has been coming less and less too, afraid to enter the Wood without meeting me at the river first, no doubt still spooked by our encounter in the dark. I would assure her that it won't happen again, but maybe it is for the best. She must have a life beyond this, a family at home wondering about her. Rosalind never asks me where I go, and I offer no explanation. There is no good answer to give.

Spring is growing near. Hard to tell in our perpetual darkness, but there is a thawing deep underground, and a freshness in the breeze, carrying the outside world to me where seasons still hold sway. Soon, the sun will return with the eternal days and twilight nights that I've grown to love in my interment. I wonder if Rosalind will like them too.

That thought haunts me throughout the day, and makes me leave Rosalind early, too nervous to talk. I walk through the dark trees, seemingly aimlessly, but then the afternoon sun shines low and bounces off the river, subdued in the midst of winter. She is there, sitting under our tree, looking down to where the river winds out of sight. I sit beside her, and she instinctively reaches out and strokes my head behind my horns. I purr.

"I think I know this river from before, when I lived in the city. It was a dark and awful night, and I ran into the Wood, trying to get away from my life. I touched grass barefoot for the first time that night."

I remember. Her hand slips down my face, across the healed scar, to scratch along my jaw line.

"Ever since, through all the turmoil of my life, my home, my family, this place, the Wood, has felt right. Never the same, but always right."

I'm glad she feels that way. Sometimes it fits like a second skin, but more recently, I've felt like an unwanted guest.

"Do you wish sometimes, that you could run? Just run away from everything around you until the world you know is behind you?"

Always.

She seems surprised at the quickness of my response. "Have you seen everything in the Wood? I can't imagine how long it took you to do that."

Seen enough.

She laughs, and I laugh too, a sound that could start avalanches. She turns to me, face inches from mine. "So, where would we go? I've seen cities, towns, trees and unimaginable wonders. What else is there to see?"

The sea.

She freezes, eyes bright. "The sea... I've only seen paintings. It looks... wild."

Never been.

"Neither have I."

Would you go?

"Oh, I could never go by myself, it's so far." She gives me a questioning look. "Unless... you went with me."

Now it's my turn to freeze. Leave. Leave this all behind, every miserable choice and failure that led to this point, and start anew, an animal, a monster, but free of the chains of an unfulfilled curse, forever. And to experience things anew with her, sleep under the stars at night and run through the fields by day, always by her side. A beautiful dream.

A futile dream. No matter my intentions, I'm bound here, by curses and fate, by a girl in a castle, by my own foolish choices.

I focus on her. She hasn't moved. Only a moment has passed, a breath. I slowly write, *Can't leave.*

Her face falls, but she quickly composes herself. "That's alright, I was just talking. It doesn't mean anything."

Damn it. I can't help it, I live for her happiness. I write, *Want to.*

"Really?"

Yes.

"Well then," she says, and she falls silent, staring back down the river. I curl around her back and tuck my legs under her knees, rest my head on her lap, letting my animal instincts lead me to comfort. She rests against my back, drumming soothing rhythms into my skull with her fingertips as I drift into half-sleep.

Would I go? Or was I just rambling? How often I'd thought about leaving, running away, but it had always been an abstract, an idea to toy with when the dough was unusually hard to knead, or the roof sprung a new leak. I had never voiced it, sounding petulant in my head, but it hadn't just then. The coolness of the river and the thin snowfall beyond was offset by the warmth of him around me, and I thought of how he shared my hopes that there was something else beyond this life, waiting. I traced his words in the dirt, once again wondering what kept him here, and if I could do something about it. He deserved to be free.

An eternity of wondering, and the sun had about disappeared below the trees when I woke him. I asked him to meet me in three days, the first time I had ever asked him to come. He agreed, and I headed home with thoughts of freedom on my tongue. If I could find a way to free him, maybe he could free me.

The thought of leaving, and the surety that I could not, consumes me. My shoulders ache with dawn's approach, as though they are trying to shake themselves free of winter's grasp, and my mind, similarly heavy, knows that things could not continue this way for much longer. I had played out my future with Rosalind a thousand times, asked her again and again to be my wife, my only move, born of desperation. But with her, with my girl from the river... things could be different. Things had to change.

It was in this frame of mind that I found myself saying two nights later over dessert, "Would you like to see your family again?"

Her fork froze midair, a piece of plum speared on the end. "Yes, of course!"

"Then gather your things. Pick out some gifts for your family too. We'll leave tomorrow morning."

"You're joking."

"I never joke."

"That's not true."

"Are you trying to fight this?"

She thought for a moment. "Are you sure?" Her tone throws me for a moment, like a parent confirming a child's decision, knowing they'll make the wrong one but still letting them make it.

"You have more than fulfilled the bargain your father struck, and I have indeed been reprieved of my loneliness'. Your family must miss you, and I... well, let us say that I've grown accustomed to silence." I smile at my attempt at humor.

"But then, you..." she trails off, lost in thought. I wait, trying not to twitch. "One month, like you gave Father," she says suddenly. "And then, I'll come back."

I am unnerved by this turn of events. I had not said that she had to return, and yet she chose to see it that way. Before I can try to piece together my next words, she jumps out of her seat, smiling and pacing with frenetic energy. "Yes, of course, one month should do it. I'll go pack now." She hesitates, then leans over and kisses my cheek, and bounds out of the room. Still as stone, I wonder at her words and actions, as I have done these past weeks, with little success. There were too many paths this road could take. Did she still feel bound here, by oath, or was this a sign of caring?

I haven't been able to eat or sleep properly since I left the river two days ago. As much calm preparation as I had put into my first plan to run to the Wood, months and months ago, this time I was guided by emotions, anxiously waiting with the idea of what was to come. Sleeping under the stars, riding fast as thought through the trees, and the promise of a distant shoreline and an unknown sea. I had taken to holding the blue rose at night, for comfort. It helped me sleep darker and deeper. But with my waking hours now filled with restless energy, I wore it looped around my neck, nestled in the folds of my winter clothes, to bring me what little peace it could.

My last day, I woke early to visit Ilena. I had seen less and less of her as winter deepened, but I made the soft-footed trek to her home, and she was kind enough to let me warm my numbed feet by the fire.

"You're growing soft," she said, offering me a cup of herbal tea. "I thought it was you who was supposed to be assisting me." I inhaled the rising steam, detecting mint, and took a drink. It scalded my tongue, but it shocked consciousness back into my mind, which had grown thick with cold and sleep as I'd slogged through the snow in the pale dawn.

"Winter has frozen my limbs. I should have come to see you in the spring instead," I replied, and took another drink.

"Perhaps," she said. "Then, you wouldn't be leaving already."

"Leaving? I just got here."

She only looked at me, and her face, hidden and revealed by the fire below, looked more ancient, more timeless. She seemed keeper of the knowledge of the foundation of the world, and I felt small, undeserving in a way I had never experienced in the presence of any royal or wizard. Then she moved, the look disappeared, and the Ilena I knew sat down beside me. She put her hand on mine as it rested beside me, and I knew I would no longer lie to her.

"I want to know more about the web, the ether. How do you find it?"

"I would normally say it finds you, but that's a little too intentionally vague," she said. "The best I can describe is when you're sitting in front of the fire on a dark night, and you start to drift. You are asleep, and yet not asleep, all at once. Reality works its way into your dreams, and your dreams come alive. Following the ether is like that. You see in two different directions at once, two different planes of existence, and the tug is the thread of the web. Of course," she mused, "that's how it works for me. It can be different for others. I knew of another weaver who felt it in her feet. Never wore shoes, no matter the weather, so she could better find the path." She moved into a kneeling position, and gestured for me to copy her.

"But, you said it's dangerous to follow the web."

"It can be, especially to those untrained, or those too sensitive to its influence," she said as turned up palms upward on my folded knees. "Of course, it can have influence over those whose psyches are dense as fog who wouldn't see the quicksand until it was up to their knees. A manticore will attack, whether you are aware of it's presence or not."

My mind drifts to that dark night in the Wood. "What if I get lost?"

"That's why I'll go with you now, if you go at all," she said, tilting my head back till my vision with filled with the earthen ceiling. "I don't want you to get discouraged, though. It often takes years of training to hone this skill. But you," she paused, and I resisted the urge to look over at her, "you have a spark. I could see it, the first time I saw you. And sometimes, that is enough."

I could hear her move across the room, come back, and something drop in the fire. Sparks flew past my vision, lazily drifting, at first yellow and orange, but now green, blue, white.

"Focus on loosening your body, toe to ankle to knee, head to neck to chest. Breathe deeply. Pretend you are going to sleep."

I concentrated on breathing, releasing the tension from my muscles.

"What you're searching for is a sound you can't hear. The noise that wakes you in the night, but you can't recall what it was."

I let my eyes close.

"The sound coming from inside your house when you are the only one there."

All I could hear was my heartbeat.

"When you're sure you've heard your name called on a busy street, but there is no one you recognize."

Her voice sounded so faint in comparison to the blood pumping behind my ears. I was afraid I wouldn't be able to hear anything with this racket.

"More than sound, it is a feeling, perhaps one you've felt before, but this time, don't dismiss it. Follow it."

I couldn't follow anything but my heart thumping in my chest. I tried to stay still, follow Ilena's instructions, but my neck felt tight and constricted, and I involuntarily pulled at the chain, brushing my hand against the rose.

The touch sent a shock through my spine, and I opened my eyes in surprise, to tell Ilena. But then I saw silver, thousand of glistening silver strands stretched across the earthen room, around jugs and bottles, through the fire, and positively dripping off the heartwood roots. I slowly reached out and touched one strand, and felt nothing, even though I could see it bend around my finger. I lightly pulled it towards me, and now I could feel something, nothing solid, but more like a cold breeze, or water. It slid over the back of my hand, and I watched it refract and bend around my wrist. I looked down at my other hand, the one that had touched the rose, and it was nearly eclipsed by the riot of silver erupting from the rose, twisting and curling like hair in the breeze. I inhaled a scent of water and starlight, and I was standing, moving, following the strands that ran between the outstretched fingers of my left hand, and tugged at the rose clasped in my right hand. I was nearly at the door when Ilena wove herself into the strand before me, hands extended. Her palms were illuminated, not just with the web around us, but with glowing shapes and patterns seemingly tattooed into the skin. She began to make intricate symbols in the air with her hands, gathering other strands with her fingertips and slowing weaving the thread pulling me into the web she wove between her hands. The slack strand grew tighter, the last thread connecting us broke, and I blinked as the silver glow disappeared, replaced by the dim glow of the fire. I could barely see Ilena's face in the new gloom, but I could hear her deep breaths.

"Well," she said at last, "that was unexpected." She moved around me, and I looked at my hands, searching for those silver threads.

"That was the ether?"

"Yes," she said, and I turned to see her dipping her fingertips in a small pot on one of the heartwood root shelves. In the firelight, they gleamed nearly as bright as the silver had. "You are quite a medium, Evelyn. For most, it takes years to see the ether as clearly as you did. And not just see it, but follow it. I must confess, I was a little unprepared for your aptitude, but I am glad I was here to unravel you before you went too far." She rubbed salve between her fingertips, the glistening oil fading as it absorbed into her skin. I looked down at my hands again, rubbing my knuckles, palms, wrists.

She noticed my gestures. "Not to worry, your hands are in fine shape. Mine, however, after so many years of bending and prodding the web of the ether, tend to need a little care, especially after such an... unexpected weaving." The salve had disappeared, and maybe it was a trick of the firelight, but I thought I could still see the tattooed patterns on her palms. I looked away, into the fire, still rubbing my wrists. And then, I remembered.

"I've felt that before," I half-whispered to myself.

"What?"

"The thread, the pulling, that scent...it's happened to me before! I'd forgotten, or pretended I'd forgotten," I said, "but that night, at the river..." I whirled around the room, wishing I could still see those threads, wondering how they were hiding in plain sight.

"Evelyn." Her voice was calm, even. "If you have felt this before, you know then how easy it is to get lost in it."

"I know," I said, still wondering, "but what if-"

"You would have walked until you fell from this earth." I turned to see her looking at me, looking at the rose. "Where did that come from?"

"I made it," I said.

"From what?"

"Scraps of dress, needle and thread, rose petals."

She could sense my evasion. "And where did the rose petals come from?"

I did not say, but she knew. "There is great magic bound within that," she said, reaching out but not quite touching the rose. I gripped it tight, but no silver appeared. "You've woven something, perhaps by accident. Perhaps, not so accidental." She looked into my eyes. "It wants you to go somewhere, Evelyn. It wants to lead you. It is waiting inside your quiet moments, when your mind is drifting, to suggest to you its path." She finally did touch it. "If you follow it, I do not know where it will take you."

Sitting by the front windows that night, I mulled Ilena's words over and over. She had told me not to follow the rose, to take it off and put it away. But I knew where it was leading. It was leading to him. I couldn't wait to tell him about it tomorrow, describe to him the ether, maybe try to show him.

I turned to Father, lost in reverie before the fire. I wondered if he had ever learned about the ether in his travels, but I highly doubted it. Father was a man of earth, of tactile sensations and physicality. Magic had never interested him. But, he did know other things.

"Father?"

In the first days of Rose's absence, he would have turned to me only with great effort, or he may not have even heard me at all. Even now, his current quiet contemplation worried me. But then he looked up at me with a small smile, and I was reminded of the charismatic man who held my mother's hand and commanded a hall with only his voice. "Yes, Evelyn?"

"Could you tell me about the sea?"

"The sea..."

"I know you'd been before on your travels, we only ever saw the river when we came to port to see you off."

"I remember," he said, still smiling at the memories of happier times.

"But I've only ever seen paintings of it, and as one who has seen a dreadwolf in real life, paintings of a wild thing very rarely do it justice."

I got a laugh out of him at that, quiet but earnest, so unheard in that house that Giselle peaked her head from around the kitchen doorway. I saw her looking and beckoned her in to sit beside me on the window seat.

"So, what do you want to know about the sea?"

"What it's like, what you thought of it."

"Are there truly mermaids?" asks Giselle.

"None that I ever saw, though many of the sailors would shove wax in their ears whenever they neared a particularly rocky coast." He leaned back, reminiscing. "The salt in the air, you could taste on your tongue, it coated everything in brine. I saw in the water every shade of blue imaginable. The captains seemed to treat the sea like an animal, capable of being trained, but never fully domesticated, never truly predictable."

"It has a wild heart," I said.

"Exactly, darling," said Father, leaning forward towards us. "It would even roar when storms descended."

"Were you ever afraid?" asked Giselle.

"All the time," Father said simply. "But never enough to stop me from admiring it."

He stood up then and reached for a pamphlet of papers in a shelf above the fireplace, where he kept his work things. He opened it to reveal maps of shorelines, the blue of the sea indicated in the thinnest wavy lines of blue ink. "The more we traveled, the more maps we needed," he said as Giselle and I picked them up to study them by the firelight, "since some places were at that point uncharted. I had stopped traveling with the ships for some time when these maps started coming back to me, of stops on unknown shorelines along their voyages. There were times I wished to go back out with them, be an explorer, but your mother had other plans." He drifted off, still smiling, but with an unmistakable sadness. Giselle and I looked at each other.

Giselle was bold enough to speak what we were both thinking. "Do you ever regret that you couldn't sail the world?"

He looked at us sharply and held out his hands so we could hold them. "Never, my darlings. As long as you and your mother were here, I had more than enough adventures." He rubbed his thumbs along our knuckles. "Besides, there are only so many seafaring years a man has before the sea becomes his mistress, and your mother was more than enough for me." We all laughed at that, and for the first time since I had chosen to leave, there was a hint of sorrowful doubt about what I would be leaving. It was strong enough that I couldn't sleep, and though I fitfully dozed near dawn, when the sun came up, I knew that my choice to leave was no longer so easy, if at all possible. I didn't grab my pack when I went out the door, knowing I could come back for it if I changed my mind. I set nothing in stone. I would go see him, and then I would make a choice.

As we get closer to the river the next morning, the sun begins to touch the trees. Rosalind is quiet, determined, but there is also happiness in her steps. She is being reserved for my sake, but I'd rather her be honest, as always. Perhaps it is too late for that, but I still ask, "Are you excited to see your family again?"

"Very much, I hope that not too much has changed. It feels like I've been gone a very long time, years, rather than a couple of months."

"Time can be that way here."

"I'm sure everything is the same," she reassures both of us emphatically. "Father in his chair, Giselle resting the day away in her room, Evelyn flying like a dervish through the house. She is constantly cooking, cleaning, working. I think she uses it as a means to cope with our new life, which is better than doing nothing, like Giselle." She is silent for a moment. "I wonder if they have missed me."

"Beyond doubt," I assure her. She seems to push that negative thought aside and her smile returns, along with the bounce in her step. "Won't they be surprised to see me coming through the door? Especially with all the gifts I'm bringing," and she swings the bag she packed, "though I'm sure they won't need them."

"They've been well taken care of in your absence."

She looks at me, questioning. "I've seen to it they have an endless amount for whatever they may need. Of course, it only seems endless," I say wryly. "Everything must end."

"That is very generous," she says.

"From your point of view, maybe, but from mine, I could never give them enough to replace what I took from them."

The river emerges from the trees, dimly gleaming in the light of dawn, the snow banks on the far side already melting in the faint sunlight. "I'll see you in one month, then."

"Be careful crossing the river," I say, evading her words. "Even frozen, it can be dangerous."

"I will." She lingers, the thumb of her free hand rubbing her fingers, a sign that she is thinking, considering. She suddenly reaches out and touches the side of my face, unknowingly tracing the near-invisible scar on my cheek. "I will be back." She turns and slowly but surely, crosses the river. I remain in the shadows of the tree as she reaches the other side and turns to wave.

"Rose?"

The girl at the river turned back to me, one hand outstretched from a soft sable cape, and it was Rose, hair woven up in pale pink ribbons and covered in soft blush silk, but unmistakably her. "Evelyn!" she cried as she flew into me at full speed, nearly knocking me down. I instinctively wrapped my arms around her, too many thoughts jumping for attention in my mind.

I started with the easiest. "What are you doing here?"

"I came back to see you all! I've missed you so much!"

"I've missed you too," I said into her hair, and I was astonished how much I realized I had missed her. No matter our misgivings and grudges, she was still my little sister. Perhaps absence really did make the heart grow fonder.

She finally pulled away, and I saw how she had changed, grown, her face older than I remembered, more serious. "How did you find your way back?" I asked, genuinely curious.

"He showed me that way," she said, and her eyes darted back to the river.

If I had never seen him before, I would have mistaken him for the deepest shadow. But he was unmistakable to me. He stood motionless beneath the tree where he rescued me, too dark to see his eyes.

I can't breathe. The two of them stare at me from across the river, but I barely notice Rosalind's gaze. I'm held captive by the hurt, bewildered eyes of the woman I rescued, who I now realize, too late, must be Rosalind's sister, Evelyn. Their voices are indistinguishable above the murmur of the river, but the pain of her gaze is clear. She hadn't known, all this time, that I was her sister's captor. Rosalind remains unfazed, continuing to talk to her sister, and leads her away, over the ridge and out of sight.

Rose chattered away at my side, no doubt telling me of her adventures at the castle in the Wood, but my mind was sliding, my eyes unfocused. It had been him. It had always been him, the monstrous shadow with teeth and claws that made my father trade his life for his daughter. It all made so much sense now, I wondered if some part of me hadn't known all along.

I continued to glide through life as we made it back home, through Giselle's loud shriek and Father's cries as we all embraced, a family once again. They all sat down by the fireplace, Rose continuing her account of the last few months, while I stood by the still open door, leaning against the jam for support. I dragged myself back to the present.

"He keeps a tight grip on you, doesn't he, your mysterious lord?" I heard Giselle comment, her familiar sharp wit sneaking back into the joyous reunion. "I do hope you have some jewels to show for it."

"I actually brought you gifts from him," Rose responded, guileless, and pulled from her bag a beautiful red dress with golden threads and satin and handed it to Giselle, who exclaimed over every silken detail. She handed Father a thick green velvet cloak trimmed in brown sable fur. She placed something in my hands, and I looked down to see a dark blue dress, a dress as blue as midnight, as blue as my roses, his roses. Something inside me snapped, and for a dangerous second I teetered on the edge of violent explosion. But then my knees gave, my days of meager eating and fitful sleeping catching up to me, and I slipped into unconsciousness.

I woke to Giselle pressing a damp cloth to my forehead. The early morning sun swam through the warped window, and I closed my eyes again.

"Finally," she said, pushing herself off the chair to sit by me on the bed. I rolled into her, resting my head on her knee. She stroked my damp hair away from my face, and I opened one eye to see her looking at me carefully.

"I've never known you to faint before," she said lightly, but the concern remained in her eyes. "All your hard work, you would think you'd develop a stronger constitution."

I managed to push myself up to a sitting position. "Where is Rose?" I croak.

"Downstairs with Father, catching up." She handed me a glass of water, and I drank it gratefully. "They are both in great spirits. It's quite catching, I confess I am a little happy to see her."

"Me too," I said truthfully between sips. My mind was calmer, so it was easy to lie and say that the surprise of Rose's return made me faint when Giselle asked me. She left to tell the others I was all right, and I swung my feet onto the floor, which still felt like it was slanting beneath me. Something twisted on my neck, and I found the blue rose snaking into my hair. The world tilted farther. I wanted to rip it off, tear it apart and throw it out the window, but I was unable to do more than remove it and banish it to the farthest, darkest corner of my drawer. I wrapped a shawl around my shoulders, smoothed my hair and slowly made my way downstairs, where my family sat, covered in fine fabrics and chatting energetically. The blue dress was draped over the window seat, so I sat in the armchair with my back to it. Rose smiled at me, and I smiled back. It was so easy. Our sister was back, and everything was as it used to be. I dragged my mind into the conversation around me.

"…and the library," Rose continued, "I went in it every day and always found something new to read. I swear the books moved when I wasn't looking." She laughed, and Father smiled like I hadn't seen in months.

"It sounds like the perfect place for you," said Giselle. "I'm surprised you came back at all."

"I've missed you all so much," said Rose, deflecting. But Father noticed.

"How long will you be staying?" he asked.

"One month," Rose answered quietly.

Even Giselle picked up on the sad silence exchanged. "Well, we're happy to have you home," Father said, and leaned over to hold her hand.

"Are you happy?" I heard myself ask. Rose looked back at me, her brows furrowed as if she heard something off in my voice. "I am," she said simply, and I wondered if she knew what I was truly asking, and if she was being truthful herself.

I let myself wander in and out of the conversation, happy to not be called upon. Thoughts I'd rather not entertain kept floating through my mind, dominated by black shadows. I kept a smile on my face, happy for Rose's return through the afternoon, through the sun setting behind the trees, through dinner and clean up, banking the fire and saying our good nights. I snuck to Rose's room, and I saw her sitting up in bed, her eyes illuminated in the moonlight.

"Can I come in?"

"Of course," she said, and lit a candle on her windowsill. The rose petals, that we hadn't touched since she left months ago, faintly glowed. When she saw me looking at them, she swept them up into her hand and started feeding them to the flame.

"I don't know if Father told you yet, but…I know, where you've been."

"He hadn't, but I could tell," she said. "When you first saw me, you looked like you saw a ghost. And you saw…him, didn't you? At the river?"

I nodded silently. Another petal turned to smoke.

"I know he looks frightening, but you get used to it."

How could I tell her that I was more than used to it, that I had touched those silver horns, his midnight fur.

"I try to focus on his voice."

"His voice?" He could speak this whole time. Shock and betrayal stunned me into silence.

Rose didn't notice it. "It is almost like a man, but it echoes, like thunder in a canyon. It is still the most human thing about him."

Had she never looked him in the eye? Surely she would have seen his humanity there. Another flare, another petal gone.

I regain my voice. "And are you...happy?"

"I could be," she said. "My time there is entertaining, more books than I could ever hope to read, and I've come to enjoy our nightly dinners."

"He eats with you?"

"No, he's never eaten in my presence. Maybe he is ashamed. Maybe he cannot."

I know he can.

"But I suppose he does it for me, a habit to make the castle seem more like a household."

"But does it feel that way, to you?"

"It doesn't matter much what I think," she said, and a little of my old annoyance with Rose's self-sacrifice comes tumbling back. But I forced myself to dig deeper.

"Why doesn't it matter?"

"Because he needs me." She saw my questioning gaze in the sudden flame of another petal disappearing. "He's asked me to marry him. That's why he asked Father for one of his daughters. I'm almost certain now that if Father had come back alone, he would have sent him away unharmed." She fell silent, but I had nothing to say, so she continued, staring into the fire. "He waited for months to ask. I think he's been trying to court me all this time, he even threw me a birthday party." She smiled a little at that. "I told him about your sixteenth birthday. Everything. You know, I've always regretted that night," she said, and she looked up into my eyes. "I didn't realize what I was doing, and then, it was too late. And we..."

"I was hurt," I interrupted. "Too young to be mature, too old to forgive. I let it fester. It was easier to fight, and that sounds so awful to say now, after all we've been through. But I blamed you for everything." Even as I said it, I was blaming her, but she couldn't know that yet. I couldn't talk about the present, but I could try to reconcile the past.

"I am sorry," she said.

"I'll forgive you that night, if you forgive me every night since."

She nodded, and we embraced. It felt like the beginning of an untested bridge, tenuous but hopeful, and I tried to push away the thought that I would end up burning this bridge before the month is out, the way the last of the petals were extinguished in the flame.

ELEVEN

CHOICES

I've been at the river all night. I refuse to move from under the oak where Evelyn and I made our plans to escape, where I let her sister go, where I saved her, where I betrayed her. Foolish hope lingered in my mind, telling me that if she'd only come back, then I could explain everything, find my voice and speak the words to fix every lie between us. The sun sinks, sets, rises at dawn on a frozen river, an unbreakable silence.

I can't take it. I can't count all the times I've tried to break the boundary of the river, but never has it mattered more than now. I finally move, force life into my numb legs and stand at the river's edge, glinting in the bright sunlight, perhaps the easiest of days to cross. No errant rapids, the rushing water is locked deep under a layer of clearest ice. Even the streams of bubbles are immobile. It would take no more than three great strides to cross. I could leap it if I had enough room to take a running start.

The high-pitched ringing begins to rattle in my skull. I push it back and raise a paw to place on the frozen river, only to be greeted with the sensation of a hundred bees swarming between my ears. My paw lands, and the world slips beneath me. At first, I think it is the slickness of the ice, but strange spots float across my eyes, like the bubbles below bursting into life. I can faintly feel the ice underneath my paw, and I lift another. This time, I do slip, and feel the ice crack from the blow of my jaw. I can no longer hear the world around me, only the blood racing through my body. I try to open my eyes, but the world around me runs like water on a windowpane, melting and distorted. My back legs, kicking helplessly on the bank, finally connect with earth, and I push a little forward. My stomach churns with searing pain, my head feels as though it is splitting down the middle, and a sound I recognize as myself screaming fills my ears as my front paws back-peddle furiously. The instant I'm back on the bank, the pain stops, and the only sound is my frantic breathing as I try to keep from falling into unconsciousness. I cast a wary eye at the river, quiet and still, and half walk, half drag myself over to the oak to shield myself from the blinding sunlight. Slowly, my panting subsides, and my legs recover enough to stand on, but I do not make another attempt to cross, slinking instead into the undergrowth of the Wood.

"So strange that she has only now come to visit," Giselle said as she sat in front of the mirror the next morning, braiding her hair. "It's been months with no word, then she shows up, without her gentleman, no horse or carriage. It makes no sense."

"Yes, strange. No sense," I said automatically, staring out the window.

"Now, why don't I believe it when you say it?" she said, turning around to look at me. I looked towards her, ready with yet another excuse, but her face, devoid of cunning, showed only questions, and I was suddenly tired, tired of the lies, and afraid of losing not just one, but two sisters because of my wall of secrets.

"Giselle, there are many things about Rosalind's leaving that we...that I haven't told you. For so long there has been this secret between us."

"This secret, among others," she said, but without malice, and she sat beside me and took one of my hands.

"So many secrets...I don't know where to begin."

"We have all day."

And I told her everything: the rest of Father's story, and his binding me to secrecy, the self-sacrifice of Rose, the night I fell in the river, the day I finally crossed it and met him, sneaking to the Wood day after day, seeing him more and more, until I finally saw him for what he was. Giselle asked hundreds of questions while I told my tale, but when I had finished, she was silent too. Birds flew across the window, the sun still high, and the trees whispered in the quiet.

"So what are you going to do?"

"Do?"

"About Rose, and him."

"Nothing."

"But you said she's going to marry him."

"Yes?"

"Then, are you going to tell her that you feel for him?"

"He asked her."

"That doesn't change how you feel."

"I'm not sure at all how I feel, much less after the realizations I've had in the past day."

She sighed in frustration, and I countered. "We can't all possess the unshakable certainty in everything we say and do like you, Giselle."

"I like seeing you happy, Evelyn. And every time you've come back from the Wood, what I see in you is happiness. If what you found there is the cause of your happiness, who are we to deny you it? More so, how can you deny yourself?"

I look up from the dining room table. The fire still crackles quietly in the hearth, but I'm sure the sun could have risen and set since I first stared down at my setting. I never thought I could be lonelier than the first months of my exile, but each passing day proves me wrong. I find myself keeping the routines, like my own magic spells, including sitting down to dinner each night, alone. Waiting is easy.

I thought about Giselle's questions every day, as our family grew whole, as much as we were in the city before Mother died. What previously annoyed us now inspired laughter. Work seemed easier. Even the weather was relenting, with rain more mist and sun than driving downpour, and few to no cracks in the ceiling dripping water. I even managed to forget the pain of the river's revelations, what lay hidden in my closed drawer, in the happiness of our newly reunited family. Rose had brought back new books, pristinely bound and full of crisp paper, and we took turns reading to each other as we prepared meals, Giselle cleaning dishes and Father stoking the fire. I reminded her often of how happy I was that she taught me how to read again, but she would never know how truly grateful I was that I was able to read every word he ever scratched in the dirt.

My whole life feels now like one long pause, an inhale with no exhale. I have nothing but the guilt, gnawing my insides with a hunger I cannot satisfy. The scene at the river plays over and over in my head, the fearful relief of Rosalind's departure, the reveal of Evelyn, the girl from the river, the girl that in another life, maybe... the girl who I'd unknowingly betrayed. Evelyn, I should have known. I must have known. My thoughts of running away dwindle like a dying fire. I can now admit to myself that I had been foolish to not see sooner how much more Evelyn meant to me, how the tease of a lifted curse had blinded me to my true feelings. Rosalind was sweet, kind and beautiful, but she was not who I had waited for, not who was dearest to my heart. And now, she was the only one I could wait for.

It had been several days since Rose's arrival back into our lives, and despite the happiness of our family, a dark flower bloomed in the back of my mind, the nagging need to confront him. I wanted to storm across the river and look in his eye, make him tell me why he did everything that he did. Why did he pretend he could not speak? Why did he steal my sister from us?

One evening, after dinner had been cleared and we sat around the fire, I excused myself to go draw water from the well. Giselle gave me a meaningful look, but I ignored her and stepped outside into the gathering dark, lighting my lantern as the door closed. When I passed by the front windows, the warmth of the scene inside almost made me stop, go back and let my personal feelings slip under the strong bonds of family and disappear. But I held course and entered the Wood, finding my way quickly to the river, still encapsulated in ice and snow. I sat at the bank, drawing my cloak around me, the little light of the lantern muffled in the winter air.

Surrounded by reminders of our time together, I knew that the deal he coerced upon my father, the incarceration of my sister, could be forgiven. Rose had already done so, and she had been more wronged than I. The initial shock of discovery had worn off since I found Rose at the river, and now, sitting in the snow, I knew it wasn't anger that had kept me away all this time. As I sat amidst the sharp sounds of frost-tipped leaves and creaking branches, the only real question that remained was why, when I had met him, I had ignored who he must be, and instead, became his friend.

I no longer have any sense of time passing, of the ground under my feet or the sky overhead. At what point, I wonder, am I allowed to lose hope, lose faith? How many days, how many years must pass until I finally give up, say 'no more, no more' and face inevitability? What moment of despair would finally push me over the edge? Clouds gather on the edges of the Wood. The air hangs thick with the tension of unbolted lightning. A storm is coming.

The morning of Rose's departure was a somber one, low grey clouds and the threat of rain stretching over the horizon. We sat close together, the fireplace burning low and casting strange shadows in the dim house. Even our new finery couldn't brighten the darkness.

"You mustn't think this is the end, you know," Rose said in a strained voice. "I believe I understand his enchantment now."

My father and sister's questioning gazes made her laugh. "When you're surrounded by dishware that moves by itself, and fires that start up and bank without me, it's easy to come to that conclusion."

"I can imagine," I said, secretly comparing her experiences with my own. "What do you think it is?"

"I think he is cursed to this form until certain requirements are met," she said, pacing the floor. "Ever since he first asked me to marry him, I've become more confident that his proposal, and asking Father for one of his daughters, are important steps that he can take towards breaking his curse. He doesn't talk about his past, so I can only guess at that, but his surroundings would suggest someone from privilege. I believe a powerful enemy cursed him to this form. But it has an out, of course, every curse has an out," she said nearly laughing. "The first time I refused him, he was gone for a day, and I feared that my refusal was a blow that could have destroyed him, made the curse irreversible. If I'd had more warning before he asked, I might have..." She paused, lost in her own thoughts, and I struggled to push aside my growing dread. "But then he came back, and I now guess that he needs to take a wife, which will give him an heir, and assert his power over his domain. If I say yes, it could be enough to break his curse, and he'll be returned to his former self." She turned to us, cheeks flushed, smiling with the success of her conclusion.

"So, will you say yes?" asked Giselle, with a poignant glance at me.

Only then did her smile fade. "I probably will."

"But you don't want to."

"I told you, he needs me. It is the right thing to do. And he has been trying, for all his shortcomings, to make it easy ‑ creating a beautiful place to stay, pleasant conversations and nightly dinners, courting me with presents and compliments. If I don't, who knows how long he'll remain there as prisoner? Even now, I fear a month may have been too long to be gone."

I'm baffled at her stubborn determination. "Have you told him how you feel?" I asked, my own feelings running high.

"It runs the risk of revealing what I know about the curse."

She was right about that. From what I had learned, it was unwise to let a curse know how much you know, even more so if you're trying to break it. Curses could be vindictive on more than their intended targets.

"Rose, I don't like this," Father broke his silence. "It's not your fight, and you could get hurt. And what if you're wrong? Why don't you just stay here with us? The last few weeks have been so lovely."

She shook her head with a sad smile. "I might still be able to see you all. You could come visit after, there are plenty of rooms for you to stay in."

"But you don't love him!" I cried out.

She squared her slight shoulders. "Sometimes, we have to sacrifice in order to do what is right."

I was torn between fury and agony. I couldn't help the tears that painfully rushed to my eyes as I grabbed her hands. "Just stay here one more day, please! Just stay." I felt Giselle close behind me, her hands on my hands, begging with clenched fingers. Father knelt behind Rose, one arm around her shoulders. She gave in quietly. "One more day."

In the middle of the night, I suddenly awoke with a sense of dread. What if that wasn't his curse? I sat up, pressing my fingers to my eyes, listening to the remnants of the day's thunderstorm slide off the roof. The quiet noise threatened to send me back to sleep, but I could not let this thought slip away as most dreams do. What if agreeing to marry him meant nothing? As far as curses go, the solution seemed too simple, too easy, especially after the trouble it must have been to cast it. And why did his curse permit him to request my sister's hand in marriage, if that truly was his one salvation?

My thoughts churned as I worked through each step, remembering all Ilena had told me. Curses seem a passion play because they are meant to teach, in their own twisted way. If this was meant to teach a lesson, what lesson had Rosalind learned? To give in to demands? To obey duty over love? To be sure, there was a sacrifice in facing the unknown, which she had done, but if that were the case, how had she changed? She was still the same Rose we'd always known, still concerned with others feelings above her own, often annoyingly so, and the moral stronghold, both mature and immature.

Beyond that, what had...*he* learned? He'd made a devil's bargain with my father, brought my sister into his home with the intention of making her his bride, and then...let her go? And in the midst of it all, he had saved me, and I had grown to love...

Rose was right, he was trapped. But she needed something else to end this curse, and if she didn't have it, the results could be disastrous. I had to prolong her stay, and hoped to solve this curse before she returned without the proper weapon. I ran to her room, without thought of keeping quiet, ready to wake her and tell her everything, anything, to get her to stay. A small, screaming part of me knew it was already too late before I saw the empty bed, the snuffed candle. "Damn you, Rose," I forced my curse down to a strained whisper, and flew back to my room. Giselle stirred as I grabbed a pair of boots from under the bed.

"What's wrong?"

"Rose is already gone. Didn't even wait till morning. Probably trying to prevent another scene like today. Damn it, why won't these boots fit?"

"Most likely because those are mine," she said, coming around the side of my bed to grab my shoulders. "Evelyn, calm down. There's nothing you can do."

"I'm not going to let my sister get hurt," I said as I tried to throw her off.

"Neither am I. You don't know what you're walking into. This curse sounds serious."

"Rose needs me. And even if she doesn't, she needs to know. I should have told her everything the first day she came home." I rolled backwards off the bed and landed on my boots. In a flash they were on, before I fastened my cloak. My gaze lingered on my closed drawer, closed for a month against things I'd rather not face, but now must. I pulled it open and my fingers easily found the rose, like it was searching for my touch. I hung it about my neck. "You can't stop me, Giselle. I have to do this."

"This is foolishness!" Giselle cried. Then she picked up her discarded boots and pulled them on. "Of all the ridiculous things to do..."

"What are you doing?"

"Coming with you, you impetuous child. Wait, where are my gloves?"

"You can't be serious."

Giselle ignored me, and pulled her gloves out of her drawer with a triumphant flourish. "You should put on a pair too, you'll catch cold."

"Giselle, you can't come with me. Who will look after Father?"

"I have no doubt that we'll be back soon enough, and if we aren't, I'll be even more glad I decided to come along. Here, my old gloves should fit you."

"You'll slow me down, you're not familiar with the Wood."

"Good thing I have such an experienced guide," she said as she finished the clasp at her throat, and walked towards the door, holding out a pair of gloves for me. "Are we going now?"

I was torn between frustration and relief, and settled with a peeved look as I walked by her and snatched the gloves. "Try and keep up."

"Whatever you say, little Evelyn," she said in a chipper tone behind me.

I hear birds singing in the eternal predawn, waiting for a sun that hasn't been seen in months. How long has it been since I moved from the front doors, lying on the marble floor as the eternal night combats the warm light of a hundred candles behind me? The spirits here remain as optimistic as the birds, keeping a tidy home, waiting for her return. It has been an eternity since she left. The urge to hunt, repressed for untold days, boils under my skin. Hunger all but consumes me. I am loathe to leave, in case she does come back, but when I hunt, I forget my past, my humanity, all the pain I have felt and inflicted upon others. It is just the chase, the prey, the sweet oblivion. I run to the Wood.

I was a little surprised at the deftness with which Giselle made her way behind me through the treacherously slick undergrowth of the Wood, with only the dim light of the approaching dawn to assist her. "And here I thought years of dance training would have no practical application in our exile," she said lightly, gracefully sidestepping a tree root while handling a low tree branch like the hand of a waiting partner. "Now, where are we going?"

"Across the river."

"And then what?"

"We'll see."

"I'd feel more comfortable if you at least pretended you had a plan."

I sighed with exasperation as droplets of water found their way from the leaves overhead onto my face. "The *plan*, then, is to find Rose before she finds the Beast. This curse is more complicated than she knows. Once we have her, we'll figure out how to break it."

"So, the plan…is to make a plan."

"Yes."

"Maybe I should just stop asking questions."

I was ready to retort, but we broke through the last line of trees and came upon the river, surging with new life, swollen with melted ice and rolling as fast as wind.

"Does it always look like that?" Giselle asked hesitantly.

"If you were going to stop asking questions, now would be the time," I cautioned as we approached the river. The ground was slick and treacherous, and we held each other's hands till we stood at the rocky outcropping where I normally crossed. The path of rocks across was half drowned, and for the first time since deciding to follow Rose, I faltered. But I forced a deep breath, and realized that if Rose had made it across, surely we could too. I reached into my pack and pulled out the coil of rope. "I'll cross first. That way, you can see where I step. Then, tie the other end around yourself, and I'll anchor the rope to the tree so you can cross. Unless, of course, you'd like to go home now."

"Don't push me, little Evelyn, or I might do just that," Giselle said as she took one end of the rope. I looped the other end across my chest, took a steadying breath, and stepped into the river.

The water leapt up and coiled around my ankles like serpents, biting with ice-cold water that soaked the leather and chilled me to the bone. I heard Giselle's voice above the roar of the river, shouting in what I hoped was an encouraging tone, and I found myself whispering under my breath, *you will make it, you will make it, you will make it* and then the ground rushed up to meet my outstretched hands, and I have made it across. I stood up breathlessly and turned to see Giselle tying the rope around herself, and I quickly walked once, twice, three times around the big oak tree and tied it off low so I could grab it if something happens. But Giselle again surprised me, as with careful steps and steadying pauses, she landed on the shore beside me.

"Well, that was exhilarating!" she said as we untied our respective knots. "I'm glad I took it slow, even though you made it look like nothing."

"What do you mean?"

"You flew across the river. It didn't even look like you touched the rocks."

"Practice, I suppose," I brushed it off. "You didn't do half so bad yourself." The rope went back in its pack. "Hopefully, that will be the hardest part of our journey," I said encouragingly as I slipped off my cloak, now heavy with rain and river water. Giselle followed suit and we draped our cloaks over the oak tree branch, inhaling the warmer air as we walked under the dark trees.

Another faded scent leads to a dead end. I grow more and more angry, the frustrations of a hungry animal boiling in my brain. The more I try to lose myself to the hunt, the more my humanity clings to me like a spider web. I know I should return to the empty castle, the open doors, the waiting, but I feel dread seeping into my bones, unable to conjure enough rage to dissipate the horrid sinking feeling that I have failed, this time for good. I roar and pray for oblivion.

And then, a voice. Small, faint, less than a whisper from acres away, but calling me, calling me home. I run.

We had been walking too long. Nothing seemed familiar, no stone monoliths or giant heartwood tree or serene glen, just more ancient trees crowding around us, hindering our progress. The Wood remained dark in pre-dawn light, the sun forever about to crest the horizon. I could barely see them in the dim, but the beat of the heartwood roots was erratic, too fast. I finally had to stop, not because I was tired, but because I had no idea whether walking in any certain direction would bring us closer to our destination. Giselle, for her part, managed to keep her shallow breathing even, disguising her weariness. I turned around in a slow circle, forcing myself to calm down and think. I just need something, anything, to follow.

"What I'm searching for is a sound I can't hear," I whispered to myself as I closed my eyes, and leaned my head back. I concentrating on breathing, forcing my mind to clear and slip away from here, from consciousness. "More than a sound, a feeling," I murmured as my heartbeat hung thick in my ears. "I just have to…" I touched the rose around my neck, and opened my eyes. "Follow it."

The dim of the Wood had vanished and turned to silver starlight. The ether stretched around us, winding and weaving through the trees. The rose shone like a beacon.

"Follow what?" I heard Giselle ask. I turned to see her staring around us, unable to see the silver arcing around her. On impulse, I stretched out my hand, cupping one of the strands, and brought it near to touch her wrist. She gasped, staring at her hand.

"What did you just do? I…I felt something, something cold, and for a second…it glowed. What is it?"

"It's going to lead us to Rose," I said, and the thread that had been surreptitiously winding itself around my wrist tugged as I followed it into the undergrowth. Even with our mysterious guides, I did not know how far away the castle was, or if we would get there before Rose did. Silence lay as thick as fog. Even our footsteps were muffled.

Then, from far away, a roar, long and loud and familiar. It was him. I called out without hesitation, as loud as I could, and started to run, vaguely aware of Giselle keeping pace behind me. Within minutes, a sudden spear of stone and windows jutted up above the trees, a tower, and at the end of a long path, a great gate. I nearly laughed in relief. We were almost there.

I break through the tree line, panting quickly, hoping against hope. Someone is standing at the open front door; head turned away, face in shadow. Then they turn.

"Rosalind," I say breathlessly, halting. "You…"

She puts up a hand. "I said I would return. And now that I have, I would like to answer your question."

A black shape ran far ahead of us. "It's him," I said breathlessly.

"Then maybe we aren't too late," Giselle said faintly.

"Question?"

"The one you have asked me every night since my sixteenth birthday. The one that keeps you trapped here. Ask me." Her breathing quickens, her shoulders tense. "Ask me now."

"Wait!" I cried as we continued to run, but my voice was stifled by exhaustion. I tried to go faster, as fast as I had crossed the river. The wind in my hair picked up, throwing it across my eyes. The rose tapped a metronome against my breastbone. They were so close. "Wait!"

I can't process what she asks of me. Rather, I don't want to. I know that I should ask her. I asked her for months, there is no reason not to, now that she has come back to me of her own accord. My chance is finally here, to take a wife and return to humanity. A faint cry rings in my ears, like a memory, but I can't place it. I can't turn away from Rosalind, who is waiting, expectantly, anxiously, the tips of her fingers drumming a pattern on her folded arms. It is time.

"Please, don't!" I screamed till my throat ached, but neither he nor Rose saw me, heard me. I couldn't even hear Giselle behind me anymore, but I couldn't turn around. I had to keep running. The gates were so close.

"Rosalind, are you certain?"

She nods. "I am. I know what I have to do."

I'm briefly confused, but relief beats it into submission, relief at the glimmer of hope erupting into dazzling light.

I pushed myself beyond exertion, my legs propelling me faster than thought. The gates were behind me, the ground a blur as I came close enough to see Rose's face, and then I heard a voice, which should be muffled but rang clear as if I stood beside him, his voice saying, "Rosalind, will you marry me?" It cut like a dagger at my breast, and I stumbled, but pressed on. There was still time, as long as...

"Yes, Beast, I will marry you."

And I was airborne, caught in the grip of terror as time stopped.

TWELVE

REDEMPTION

I was floating, arched back and limbs askew, inches off the ground as if I'd been pushed back by the wind. I looked in fascination at a leaf, suspended in its journey from tree to ground. The light cresting the trees hit the fine film of dew covering it, giving it a shiny patina as rich as gold. I wanted to touch it, but my body wouldn't respond to my requests to move. Only my eyes remained in my control, and I wrenched my gaze from the frozen leaf to the scene below me, the one I'd tried, and failed, to prevent. Rose's hands were tightly gripped around her waist, her face full of worry and dawning recognition in her eyes as they were fixed on me. I tried to say her name, tried to explain, but no sound escaped me. There was no sound at all, save for a low rhythmic rushing. It sounded like my heartbeat, but lower, softer.

I tried to move again, tried to kick, thrash, scream, something. Then, I felt something like a hand on my forehead. *Patience, child. Time will return, perhaps too soon, and I must give you what I can before that happens.*

It was as low as a whisper, but I felt no breath, no presence, save for the invisible pressure on my head. *Can...am I...where are you?*

A laugh like wind in the trees. *I am where you are, which is to say, frozen in the moments between heartbeats.*

How did we get here?

You were here already. I just caught you and...stretched the moment out so I could talk to you, and even then, the moment must end eventually. Fortunately, or perhaps not so fortunately, the timing of this place, the Wood, is reacting violently to the crack in the enchantment your sister just opened, and time is more...flexible than normal.

What crack? You mean, Rose broke the curse?

If that were the case, I would have bet on the wrong horse. Another laugh, but more like a sharp winter gale. *Your sister is very optimistic, and her altruistic quest to end this enchantment is what kept her from being struck by it instantly. But, while she definitely dealt it a great blow, it is still there.*

There was a nudge on my head, and I suddenly saw him, a few yards away from Rosalind and his back to me as he reared. Only, it was no longer just him. He was splitting like a lightning-struck tree, glowing, face turned back towards me in agony as a man pulled away from his chest. Both man and animal were frozen in primeval roars, bound together by the stands of ether. I looked at the man, teeth exposed in a grimace, high cheekbones and strong chin, the deep plunging eyebrows over eyes I could now see slowly opening.

His moment is not as long as ours, but he is powerful, and moving fast.

But I saw the faint scar on his cheek, and when his eyes opened, I already knew.

This was his curse.

A sigh like leaves falling. *Perhaps it is my own stubbornness, but I never saw it as a curse. I saw it as an opportunity. But I have grown since then, and having seen what became of him...I never meant him any pain.*

As the man grew more whole, the animal began to peel, like a skin, curling in on itself till it turned more shadow than flesh. The ether stretched, strained. A few strands broke.

What will happen to him?

He'll lose his heart. All the curse did was give him the form of an animal. He is the one who never let his heart be whole in what he was, and now that he and your sister have sworn an oath of duty, rather than love, the curse will take his heart, along with the animal side, and leave him. I do not know where it will land. If it chooses your younger sister, it may well kill her in rage. I don't hold much hope for your elder sister, either.

I tried again furiously to escape my confinement, rage brimming in my brain.

Don't struggle, time is coming fast enough.

No! My sisters! I won't let them die! I won't!

The last of the ether broke, and the shadow of the being I had known was now completely free of the man, who stood tall, handsome, and empty. Within the darkness pulsed a gentle glow, and I could see one strand of ether, finer than silk, tethered between it and the rose at my chest. I now understood the low rushing sound I had heard was not my own heartbeat, but the Beast's heart, and it was fading.

Give it to me.

What?

Give me his heart.

Darling girl, it is too late. And even if his heart survives, you will then be cursed, just as he was, until it too overtakes and destroys you.

The shadow hovered above us all, the glow of his heart ever fainter. And slowly, but surely, I saw it turn towards Rose, still frozen, unaware of what was coming for her, eyes still fixed on me. I must have imagined the look of calm slowly descending on her, as if she knew what she had done, and was prepared to accept her fate, if it could keep us, her sisters, safe. I must have imagined it, but it gave me strength, strength enough to finally make a sound, the smallest word, that echoed in the silence. "No."

It turned back to me, glowing brighter, and the echo of my refusal reverberated in my ears, as I said, stronger, "No."

Be strong, Evelyn. This curse has a life of its own now.

The tether between us grew taught as it inexorably came to me. The shadow reached my outstretched hand and latched on, wrapping around me like water. I couldn't see anymore, but I could feel the cool ether inside it, and I strained to wrap my fingers gently around it. I trembled as I brought it close and held it to my chest. I heard her, faintly, through the roaring in my ears.

You don't know how long I've watched him, and who he has become with you…perhaps I was wrong. Perhaps you have the strength after all.

Then there was a blinding pressure in my spine, and fire rolled under my skin. I could feel the hollow places in my body filling, stretching into unrecognizable forms as bones cracked and realigned. I wished for death with every painful breath. And then, my breathing came deeper, full of scents I had never experienced, and my limbs felt heavier, but right, as if I'd always wished I could stretch them into this new configuration.

You've contained it. A surprised statement, like a drop of water in a still pool. *I wonder from where your strength comes. Is it for your sister binding herself to a man without a heart? Or, have you finally given into the demands of your heart, and what it wants? Are you fighting for your sister, your beast, or yourself? Regardless, the curse remains unbroken. And soon, it will break you. Then again, I've already been surprised once today…* The voice was even less than a whisper, and fading fast as I struggled to open my eyes.

Wait. I have to know. Is it possible to keep two hearts alive?

More felt than heard, the voice said, *Hearts are meant to be given…*

My eyes finally opened, and Rose's calm face, the handsome man, the castle overhead and the courtyard underneath, had all been leeched of color, frozen in shades of grey. And then, I roared.

"Evelyn!"

Giselle's voice cut through my roar, and I turned to see her finally entering the courtyard, looking rather worse for wear. Her dress was missing the bottom three inches of hem, and her hair, normally so carefully placed, had escaped its braids in a flurry of waves. I stifled a laugh. "You look a little worse for wear."

Giselle had always been taller, but as she slowly approached me, she had to look up to meet my gaze. "You are one to talk."

A twitch behind me turned my head, and I saw a long grey tail, bright like starlight, slowly waving. It was connected to an animal's body. My body. I felt the talons, my four feet on the ground, ears moving independent and unfamiliar scents flooding my nose. My rational, human mind balked for a moment, and then I smelled the rose, still hanging around my neck, familiar and unchanged. I remembered what I chose, what I had to do.

"Giselle," I said, and now I heard the new timbre of my voice, "you have to go, it's not safe here." I leaned in close, and she flinched. I paused too, suddenly unsure of this body and what it was capable of. "I don't want you to get hurt."

She hesitated, then put out a hand and ran it along my back, and the anxiety fell away. "I'm not sure anything could hurt me with you looking like this. Perhaps I'll grow wings and fly away, seems just as likely to happen today as anything else I've seen." She looked past me at the doorway. I turned to see Rose walking forward. "Evelyn? Is that you? What...what happened?"

"The curse ricocheted," I said simply, shrugging my shoulders.

"Oh no, I never meant for this to happen," she said as she rushed forward and placed her hands on the sides of my new face. "That's why I left, so nothing would hurt you. This is my fault."

I laughed like thunder, confidence flooding my mind. "You're correct, but you were just doing what you thought was right." She still looked stricken, her bright hair illuminated in the rising sun, and a memory from my childhood came flooding in. "I know that sometimes, you want to just get to the end of the story, just do be done with it. But we have to keep going through, page by page, even if things are bad.”

“Then, at the end,” she said slowly, remembering, “you’ve earned the victory, or learned from the defeat.”

“I’ve learned from my defeat, and now, maybe, we can have our victory.” My sisters looked up at me, pale grey through eyes that couldn’t see color, but they smelled like they should, and I felt those bonds between us, of blood and tears and smiles, everything we had together that could never be torn apart. “You two need to get somewhere safe. We have one more problem to deal with before the day is out.”

As if on cue, he rose from where he had been crouched on the ground. Dressed in finery and draped in jewels, he stood tall, a lost prince returned from exile, his fine face still, emotionless. His beauty was almost painful to me, because he was everything I thought I wanted, and had nothing of what I had come to need. My sisters grew still at his gaze.

“Go, now,” I urged them, and placed myself between him and them as they retreated to the trees. His head tilted to one side, stiffly, like a forgotten gesture.

“I know I look different now, but do you remember me?”

“I don’t believe so.” His voice was rich like honey, but devoid of tone.

“I think you do. I’ll just have to remind you.” I took a step towards him, and felt my bones shift, settle. The hunt had begun.

“You will have to tell me later. I have to find my wife. We are to be married.”

“I’m afraid that will have to wait, until you and I speak.”

“I will have her.” Emotionless and cold, his threat still landed heavily.

“Perhaps,” I said, calculating my next move. “You are correct, you do have to find something, something which you have not had in a very long time, something that will finally end this curse.”

“What curse? I am human again. That is all I need.”

“You are still missing something.”

“A wife.”

“A heart.”

He paused, and I felt a faint reverberation in my chest. He was still here.

He laughed. It set my teeth on edge. “Why would I need a heart? What has a heart ever done for me? I had a heart, long ago, and all it served was to hurt me, break me, make me weak. I have no use for a heart."

"That's not true."

"Who are you, to know anything about me?" His cruelty bit me. "An animal, a monster, alone and cursed-"

"Just as you were." I needed to press my advantage soon. As his heartbeat grew stronger, mine began to wane. "I know everything about you."

"Very well, then in what kingdom did I grow up? When was I born? What is my real name?"

"I know that you saved me from the river, that you learnt to read and write as you are, and taught yourself how to swim. I know you run faster than thought and softer than shadow. I know you've been alone for a very long time, and I know that you forced my father to part from one of his daughters because you thought that she could save you. And she tried. Rose tried so hard, but she didn't know what you truly needed to be free from your curse, because you didn't know what you truly needed. But I do, now."

For the first time, he didn't respond. He stared, and his eyes, so familiar, twitched, an involuntary gesture in an otherwise perfectly controlled body.

"I know you need your heart, because you can't love the heartless. I know that you have a heart, because it is beating in my chest. It is now a part of me that I couldn't remove with a blade. But it, and I, will die soon, torn apart and left a shell, just like you."

"Who are you?" he asked slowly, a question dredged up from the depths.

My vision wavers, but I stood firm, a tree you couldn't uproot. "Just a girl who loved a beast. And now, before she dies, she has to tell the Beast something, something she's known for a long time, longer than was fair to keep silent from him, and herself. That...she loves him. I...love him."

"She loves him." My vision cleared, and his eyes were shining. Or maybe those were my own. I nodded. "And he loves her."

My breath caught in my throat, and though time didn't stop, the moment did stretch, and I heard his voice, the deep, animal voice, inside my head.

I do love you, Evelyn. I'm sorry for all the lies, the betrayal, every wrong thing I did that led us here. You are right, I fought the love I had for you because I didn't want to be hurt again. But, I've never hurt so much as I have these last few weeks from missing you so much, and knowing I may never see you again. And what you've done...for me...it was never your responsibility to save me.

I am trying to save you because I love you. We owe each other nothing. You should know, though, I will die shortly. I can't keep two hearts to myself.

Please, give me yours.

I can't do that to you. Not unless it is what you truly want.

But what do you want?

Well, I would like to not die.

Yes, and what else?

I want you, the you that I met so long ago, the you I fell in love with, and I'll love him no matter what form he, or I, may find ourselves in.

That is more than enough for a man with no heart.

In my last moment of consciousness, as time sped up and a shadow containing both our hearts threatened to pull away from my body, we leapt towards each other, hands and paws outstretched. We smashed together, a blur of fur and flesh as our hearts melted and combined and sank into our chests. The shadow screamed and burned like fire, but we roared back, proud and sure and full of love, and the curse shriveled into ash and smoke and then, nothing.

I open my eyes to see human eyes in an inhuman face, fur as silver as the stars. "You are still as beautiful as the day I saw you by the river, when you took off your shoes and danced in the grass."

"You were there?" Her brows knit, then smooth as she laughs, her gestures familiar even in this new form. "Why didn't you say something?"

"Oh yes, I'm sure that would not have ended in disaster," as I bare my sharp teeth and wave my paws in front of her face. She bats them aside playfully with her own, and I'm suddenly urged to touch this new face of hers, feel her fur against my skin. And then, suddenly, I am, hands appearing where before there were none, and she growls in surprise, falling back. I sit up to see skin roll up my arms, across my feet as my ankles shrink and settle above my heels.

I look up in amazement, but Evelyn is going through her own changes, smooth skin pulled tight over her collarbones as her hair pulls back and falls in waves around her flattening face, smoothly transitioning from silver to copper. Colors that I thought lost to memory become vibrant and alive again as we each watch the other transform from animal to human, clothed in simple dress, soft like velvet, or fur, hers white as starlight, mine black as midnight. Around our collars is a pattern of blue, dark as shadow, in the shape of rose petals.

"Well, that's new," I muse, looking in astonishment at my human hand. "At least, new to me. I haven't seen my own hand in...I can't remember how long. Decades, maybe."

"They do tend to grow on you," she says, but she's not looking at her hands. She approaches me slowly, warily, like I'm still an animal. She stares intently at my face. "He's still there, you know. Just below the surface, in your nose, your chin, your eyes..." She trails off, eyes widening, and puts her hands on my face as I feel my jaw line rearranging, horns pushing up through my skull, changing again. "Even more so now," she says, laughing a little.

I'm too afraid to laugh. "What does this mean? Am I still cursed?"

"I don't think so," she says, and slowly her hair recedes, turning starlight grey over elongating eyes. "If I were to hazard a guess, I would say that we have become something more than human, or animal. I don't think that we broke the curse as cleanly as intended. I am no sorcerer, though, so for a more thorough analysis, you will have to wait." Her hands are still on my face, and with her calming words, I find myself relaxing, horns retracting, jaw line smoothing. "I wouldn't dare speak on your behalf, but I am very glad my beast didn't entirely leave me with just a handsome stranger in his place." She smiles cheekily. "Though I suppose it wouldn't hurt to get to know him too."

"But...what about you, Evelyn? What you've done for me..."

"Was freely given. To be truthful, it actually feels...sort of right." As she talks, her human body gracefully pours into a beautiful creature, four-legged and fierce, covered in beautiful starlight fur, with two silver horns emerging from behind her perked ears. Her voice is lower, resonant, like water. "And if you can still love me this way, as I hope you do, then we will consider ourselves perfect and no more shall be said on who did what for whom. As long as you, too, are happy."

I let myself embrace the animal side I've so long let control me into oblivion, or beat back in hatred. "How could I not be? You have given me everything, more than I thought possible, and now...to see you like this..." I walk on four legs to her, and we don't have to look up or down to stare each other in the eye. "You are right, I still see you, just below the surface."

Then I notice it, a darkening of the glistening grey of her fur around her neck to blue, deep as shadow, in the center of her throat. She casts me a questioning look. "Around your neck, there is this blue," I explain, then stop. "Blue..." I look up at the pale green leaves in the sunlight, the brightening sky with streaks of pink and purple clouds fading into blue. "I can see the colors, again...before I even met you, all color was lost to me, but now…I can see a necklace of blue and grey woven throughout your beautiful silver fur."

"You have the same, I believe," she says.

"Really? You can see the colors too, then?"

"Yes, of course," she says, but her brows knit together in thought. "Now that you've reminded me, when I first changed I couldn't see any colors either. Everything was changing so fast all at once though, I barely registered it." She focuses on me again. "Did you mind, seeing everything in grey?"

"I grew accustomed."

"Is it so different now?"

"Yes. I had grown used to seeing you that way, and now, I have two new versions of you to recognize. But," and I touch my nose to hers, "no matter what shape you take, your eyes remain the same soft grey I've come to know and love."

We are silent for a moment, lost in time. Then she stirs. "I may actually know what changed our fur to blue. I was wearing the rose I had when we met, one of the many you gave my sisters and I. It must have gotten entangled in whatever we let loose, and now, it's a part of us."

"The roses will bring you together…" I murmur, astonished at the deftness of the curse that once trapped me, and now bound me and the woman I love together.

"What?"

I shake my head. "There is so much I have to share with you."

"Well, can you walk and talk? I'd like to catch my sisters before they get irrevocably lost."

What joy it was to run! A million interesting scents filled my nose as we flew through the trees, while two prominent ones led us quickly to my sisters arguing by the river, under a very familiar oak, about which way they ought to cross. Our sudden arrival caused some panicked chaos, before they recognized us and nearly fell down in relief as we quickly transformed into our human selves. Then it was just a muddle of voices as questions overlapped over explanations, surprise and wonder, apologies and forgiveness at what had happened to all of us.

Finally things calmed down enough for a small silence to fall as we sat below the oak, digesting the past few hours. Rose put a hand on mine.

"Evelyn…I don't think I can thank you enough."

"Neither can I," said a half-familiar male voice behind me, with an accompanying hand on my shoulder.

"Well, in all honesty, Evelyn owes me more than a few thanks," said Giselle glibly.

"Evelyn!" said Rose sharply, and I laughed.

"No Rose, she's right. Without Giselle, I may never have realized how I truly felt about you...and him," I said quietly, putting my free hand on his. "Thank you Giselle."

"Anything for you, dear sister," she said, and stretched her arms above her head. "Now, shouldn't we be getting on home? We did leave Father without a note, and to wake and find all three of his daughters gone might put him on edge."

"Father!" said Rose. "Of course, we've been gone for hours, he must be missing you both."

"Also, it is probably time that Father meets the Beast in this new capacity," said Giselle.

"I hadn't thought of that," I said, turning around to face him. "I mean, I knew we were going to have to go home eventually, and of course we'll have to explain everything to Father, to make him understand why you did what you did, and that we are all very happy at how things turned out, and that he no longer needs to be afraid, or angry, or..." I trailed off, suddenly exhausted. "We just outwitted a curse not an hour ago, and yet I think talking to Father will be the hardest thing I've done today," I said wearily as I looked back at my sisters.

Giselle smiled sympathetically. "The man is set in his ways, but it has to be done."

"Yes," said Rose. "We owe him an explanation. But, perhaps, maybe it is best if I do it." She smiled slowly at me. "I think it would be wisest if just Giselle and I go home now and break the news. Better to catch him in a good mood at the return of his youngest daughter home, before telling him his second eldest is now a shape-shifter engaged to the creature that tore his family apart for the past six months."

"You may be right, Rose," said Giselle slyly. "It could take hours, days, for us to set him right and be as glibly unconcerned about this turn of events as we are."

"Indeed," said Rose cheerily. "So perhaps, Evelyn, you should just take a week away from home, while we sort everything out. I believe there is a vacancy in a beautiful castle not too far from here," she said to him now, with only a hint of wistfulness in her voice, and none in her eyes.

"I believe that is true," he said, and took my other hand in his.

"Perfect!" said Giselle, and stood up. "Now, if you'll excuse me, I need to change out of this dress as soon as there is hot water ready for my feet." I stood up too, and we embraced.

"You be a good little beast now," she said in my ear, and I laughed, letting the animal come through in a low rumbling undertone. She chuckled as she gave one more squeeze, and then pulled away, crossing the river slowly.

While Evelyn says goodbye to Giselle, Rosalind comes up to me.

"I suppose this is goodbye, for now," she says. "I will be back sometime soon though, to finish every book in that library just like I promised myself."

"I have no doubt you will succeed," I say, smiling easy in my regained human form. She returns it, one of the few genuine smiles she's ever given me. "I suppose it is too late now to apologize for coercing you to come stay with me."

"It is never too late," she says. "But knowing why makes it easier to forgive you, as does my sister's happiness."

"I will do everything in my power to keep her happy."

"I know you will. I've seen you do it before," she adds offhandedly, but with a sad smile. "I want you to know," she says quietly, but clearly, "I did care for you. Not as much as my sister does, but in something that I could have mistaken for love. I thought I could... I tried..."

"I know," I say simply. "It was the same for me."

She takes a deep breath, and then smiles, and I feel we are companions, as though our relationship was supposed to be that way all along. "I guess we were lucky Evelyn was there to save us," she says.

"Beyond fortunate," I agree wholeheartedly as I see Evelyn turn back towards us. We walk over to her, and Rosalind takes her hands.

"Are you sure you want to talk to Father alone?" Evelyn asks.

"I've been gone from home for six months. Even arguing will be a nice change of pace," Rose says. "Don't worry about me, I've plenty to distract him with. I want to be a sister you can depend on."

"An interesting idea," she muses, smiling. "But I like it." They wrap each other in a fierce embrace, and when they pull apart, they both have tears in our eyes. She wipes them away, still smiling, and gives me a final, small nod before crossing the river and following Giselle out of sight.

I turn to look down at Evelyn, and brush her tears away. "How are you feeling?"

"Good," she says, reaching up to hold my hands on her face. "Drained, but good."

"Would you like to come back with me, and rest?"

"That sounds wonderful," she says, pulling my hands down to her waist. "But only for a little while. We have to start planning, and packing."

"For what?" I ask, our faces inches apart as I pull her close.

She says nothing, but smiles, and kisses me, and it is nothing short of ecstasy as we melt into each other, shifting without thought into slick beasts that run into the cover of the Wood.

EPILOGUE

Sunrays, tiny fingers of warmth, roused me through my closed eyelids. They amplified the surrounding scents: grass, trees, salt, human, and then animal. I opened my eyes and found him hovering over me, black as shadow, beautiful as the night. I stretched and yawned beneath him, claws extending and sheathing. Every day, this body became more and more familiar. It made most sense while we traveled – faster, durable, warm on the coldest night. There were days I wasn't human at all. But then he changed above me and I followed suit, turning on my side to look into his face as he lay beside me, propped up on one elbow.

"It still takes some getting used to, you know, seeing you like that," I said, eyes still half closed. "For so long I knew you, and now…" I reached up and brushed a lock of hair out of his face. "Thank heavens you're handsome."

He growled playfully and tweaked my nose, and I fought back, pinning him down on the moss, which led to another in the long line of uncountable kisses we had accrued since our first by the river. When we finally released each other, I resisted the urge to fall back asleep and instead sat up in the pre-dawn light. "Did you sleep well?" I asked him.

"I don't believe I even closed my eyes. I've been watching you for hours." He smiled, but his nose and mouth fluctuated between predatory and human, a sign I've come to know as unease. I cast a concerned look at him, and his face settled, trying to hide his restlessness. "Go back to sleep, if you wish. I know the past couple months have been demanding. Filled with heavy conversation."

"And even heavier lifting," I agree, playing along with his distraction. "I believe it would have been easier to uproot the house by its foundations and drag it to town."

The chaotic frenzy of the last few months had begun when we had finally returned home to face Father. Even with a week to understand, polite discussion had fallen quickly into incredulous outrage and repeated explanations, while I tried, and failed, to keep the animal side withdrawn as the argument, and my frustration, grew. But then my tail, quite accidentally, knocked over a footstool, and Giselle laughed, and then Father smiled, and tea was made and most, if not all, of the ugliness was forgotten.

Once Father was on our side, and the engagement was formalized, Rose announced that she was going to enroll in the university in Meriton, a neighboring town. That had led to more fights, Father stubborn in his stance against her engaging in an activity long dominated by men while so young and inexperienced, Rose's equally stubborn confidence and desire for a new challenge, and the rest of us wisely avoiding the conversation all together. In the end, Father again conceded, and Rose enrolled. By the time Giselle announced a month later that she wanted to move to town with Rose, yearning for more society than our home for the last few years had offered, Father was ready to agree with anything, and, in truth, was greatly relieved that what his eldest daughter wanted was what he himself had been hoping to do since Rose moved away. Soon, the home that had been refuge in our exile was empty, nothing but walls and empty rooms. For a while, I thought of keeping it, our first home together, but for all the hard work I had put into it, it held no sentiment for me.

I had asked him about the castle as our new home, but it held no love for him either, too many ghosts and painful memories. It was a place for our past, not our future. But then, before we could abandon the castle, it abandoned us, vanishing in the midst of all the chaos surrounding the last few months. We traversed the Wood searching, but never found it, though we did find in its place a giant interwoven archway, tall as the trees, of roses in every color, especially the dark ones, so black they were almost blue, held together by the russet heartwood roots. It was there, under the thorny bower, that we spent our first night together as husband and wife, and there we decided to finally leave, as we had once said we would.

Before we left, I had brought him to visit Ilena, intent on sharing with her all that had transpired since I'd last seen her. The moment she saw us both, however, she gave her little wry smile, and I knew she could see what he had been, and what I had become. She took both our hands, palms up, and after a moment I could see a glow rising up from our skin. Instead of feeling strands in the air, ether had become tattooed on our skin, encircling our bodies in a web of silver light. "I see you have found where the ether wanted to take you," she said, letting our hands go as the silver light faded. "It is too late to wonder what I could have done to better prepare you, or more effectively dissuade you," she said dryly.

"Likely nothing," I replied. "I am entirely too stubborn for my own good."

"Indeed," he said quietly, and I gave him a playful nudge.

She turned her gaze to him. "You've been on one path for a very long time. So long, you nearly lost yourself. But now," she said with a warmth I had very rarely heard in her voice before, "you now make your own path. The both of you."

I let those memories slip away as I refocused on his face, now slightly worried with a small crease between his brows. "I would not begrudge you sleep, should you desire it," he said.

"I desire a great many things," I said. "A patch of sunlight. A hairbrush, cannot believe we forgot to pack one. A grilled pheasant, with arugula and parsnips and just a hint of lemon zest." I paused, and smiled. "But your happiness is what I want most. I am ready, if you are."

He smiled too. "As long as you are with me." We gathered our packs, small but full of useful items for when we wanted cooked and seasoned food instead of raw, and after he shifted, I strapped them to his back and shifted too so we could run through the dark trees.

His unease hung on me too. For the first few days of travel, we were still learning, explorers on a quest for unknown lands. The mystery and majesty of the terrain we crossed was often enough to capture our attention. But, as happy as we were in each other, the growing fear that there was no end to our journey began to weigh on our minds. What if there was no home for us?

Then, yesterday, faintly on the breeze we caught it, a salt-swept wind that we had never encountered before. After running breakneck for hours, we had to force ourselves to get some rest, but I knew only a handful of hours had passed since we lay down. Luckily, these bodies didn't need much rest. Even now, my limbs felt fresh, the ground beneath barely a whisper as the trees flew by. His dark shadow clung to the branches, keeping pace above me as the scent of salt grew stronger, and the sound of a thousand trees stirring increased, even as the trees around us grew fewer and farther between. Soon, the branches were too small for even his light touch, and he landed beside me as we came to edge of the trees and our paws shrank into bare feet that sank into soft sand. There was a blinding flash on the horizon, and our hands instinctively found one another. As we looked, the flash of sunlight settled into a thousand mirrors dancing on a rolling dark blue mass that danced across the earth before crashing into the shore. I could taste the salt on my tongue.

"We made it," I finally exclaimed, breathless. I pulled my gaze from the sea to look at him. His dark hair danced playfully in the breeze, and his eyes were almost the same hue as the sea softly roaring before us. "Is it anything like you thought it would be?"

"No," he said softly, turning towards me. "It is much, much more."

And then we are running, shifting without thought, bounding through the sand, as the waves grow louder than our roars of delight, unafraid of the cold spray of the surf as we plunged into the sea beneath a rising sun.

ABOUT THE AUTHOR

Elizabeth Kidder is an author and illustrator, working in both fields for over half a dozen years. Previous publications include a selection of poems and short stories, both in the Artemis literary journal and in several issues of District Quarterly at the Savannah College of Art and Design, and the illustrations for the graphic novel "Jannah Station: A Soft Murder" now available on Amazon. She is currently working on an addition to an anthology of alternate history short stories, as well as a children's book about a boy who was afraid of making friends. You can view her work at www.elizabethkidder.com. She lives in Tennessee with her husband, two cats, and a collection of books that is constantly outgrowing its shelf space.

www.ingramcontent.com/pod-product-compliance
Lightning Source LLC
Chambersburg PA
CBHW070306120726
47910CB00007B/2385